I have trouble sleep _____ of the chase? It has been _____ pain to get to this point. My emotion___ ___ ranging up and down. I think of the pain, horror, and grief this man has caused his victims and their families. It needs to end tomorrow; it must.

I call P.K. again. The third time tonight. She told me to call if I needed to talk more. The woman can see inside me, I swear.

We talk more and then she says, "Please try to sleep. You need be at your best tomorrow. I want you to be with me, forever."

How did I find her? It's like it was fated. I believe it was.

I manage some sleep.

Gone But Not Forgotten

by

RJ Waters

PK & the LT, Book 2

Gone But Not Forgotten

Cover Art by *Jennifer Greeff*

The Wild Rose Press, Inc.
PO Box 708
Adams Basin, NY 14410-0708
Visit us at www.thewildrosepress.com

Publishing History
First Edition, 2021
Trade Paperback ISBN 978-1-5092-3833-0
Digital ISBN 978-1-5092-3834-7

PK & the LT, Book 2
Published in the United States of America

Dedication

This book is dedicated to my beautiful wife, Penny.
Without her almost daily reading, editing, and support,
I would be in a quagmire trying to sort this all out.

Chapter 1

Someone got away with murder tonight. It would haunt me for years.

At eleven p.m., I take to the streets to begin my shift. I'm one of two graveyard police officers and a sergeant, patrolling the small town of Morgan Hill, California.

So far, the night's been routine, a domestic dispute, a couple of drunks, and the occasional bar fight. Now it's after two a.m., and the bars have closed without any further incidents. To stay awake, I begin a security check of the businesses on my beat.

Coming out of a side street after circling a group of businesses, I pull onto the main street. A truck with a set of flatbed trailers is slowly driving in the curb lane on the opposite side of the highway. Through my open window, there is a soft warm summertime breeze, accompanied by an odd sound. It's a mechanical noise but not harsh, more like rubbing, as though something is being dragged. On the other side of the truck is an all-night gas station. The truck is between me and the gas station. I can see under the trailers, backlit by the lights from the station. Nothing is visible. The truck turns onto a side street and appears to be stopping. The driver must be hearing the noise and intends to investigate. I'll check on him if he's still here after my sweep of the district.

Continuing to the next block, I notice a car parked in the driveway of a small motel on the opposite side of the roadway. The car's lights are on, and the driver's door is open. At this time of night, the newspaper delivery drivers are stopping all over town to fill their racks. But I don't see anyone, and the car isn't one of the usual delivery vehicles. I swing my patrol car around and pull into the driveway.

It's a small blue Chevy two-door, and the engine is running. But no one's in sight.

The newspaper racks are still empty, no bundles of newspapers in the car. The motel office is closed, usual for this time of night. I turn off the car's engine and take the keys. A purse is on the floor of the passenger area. I search the immediate vicinity for a sign of anyone or anything. Negative. *What the hell.* People will leave their keys in the ignition, but women do not leave their purses behind.

My senses are on high alert, and there's a tightening in the pit of my stomach. Something's not right. I call my situation into dispatch. My backup informs me he's fifteen to twenty minutes away. Not unusual for the size of our area.

I strain my eyes, looking up and down the highway for something unusual. The driver of the car left in one hell of a hurry. Why?

Between the motel and the gas station is a vacant field. The lights of the station are bright, but the field is in total darkness. Using the spotlight on my patrol car, I drive up the curb lane scanning the field. Still nothing. Then in the glare of my headlights, I see what appears to be a clean path on the pavement. The edge of the roadway is usually covered with dirt, and loose gravel.

Something's been dragged down the road...that truck. The path continues for fifty feet or so and begins to look wet. *Oh shit.* My palms feel sweaty and gripping the wheel tighter, I pull to the outside of the trail to leave it undisturbed. The moist area gets wider and goes all the way to the corner, then appears to turn to the right. Like the truck did.

Around the corner about sixty feet away something is in the roadway. My God, it looks like a body. Driving rapidly, I radio for an ambulance, come to a halt, and hurdle myself out of my patrol car. My hand trembles as I touch the person, a woman. Damn it! She isn't breathing. I bring my hand to the neck and press my index and middle finger against the carotid artery checking for a pulse. None. I try the outer side. Still nothing. Her soft skin is warm to the touch. The woman is a Caucasian female who appears to be in her twenties. The strong odor of blood, and torn flesh, envelopes me. Nausea coils in the pit of my stomach. I must have seen this happen just minutes ago.

The truck, the damn truck.

The back of her head and torso are torn and ragged. Blood is beginning to pool under her slight frame with arms outstretched above her head, the delicate hands and wrists show deep abrasions. A rope may have been wrapped around them or somehow entangled her. A once-white blouse is shredded and filthy with road oil and muck, and her dark blue pants have been nearly ripped from her body. I'm not a novice in the emergency world, but this is overwhelming me. *Where is my backup, the ambulance, why am I alone on this barren street?*

Within minutes, which have felt more like hours,

the ambulance arrives, with my backup close behind. As the attendants rush to the body, their faces reflect the horror they're suddenly confronted with. One aide presses his hand against his mouth, as he starts to gag. He's a seasoned veteran, but the sight of her destroyed body is too much for him.

"Bob, what happened?"

"I think she was dragged by a truck." I manage to answer.

"Did you see this?"

"I think I did. I-I know I did."

"What truck, where is it?"

Then Sergeant Edwards pulls up. He'll be pissed because he was at the station drinking coffee waiting for his shift to end. "What the hell?"

"She must have jumped out of the truck and got caught in the ropes hanging off the back of the cab," speculates Jack, my backup partner for the shift.

"I bet she had a fight with the driver and tried to jump out and got hung up in the ropes," offers Les, the ambulance driver.

Tom, the other ambulance crewman, kneeling over the woman, looks up, tears forming in his blue eyes. "Bob, who would do this? What do you think?"

"Guys, I can only guess at this point, but I swear I will find the answers."

The sergeant snarls, "Social time is over. Get this scene protected. Call the coroner to come and get that body out of the street. I'll call the detective to come and take over. Then maybe I can go home and get some sleep."

Tom shakes his head. "Cold unfeeling bastard."

Dark thoughts dance through my mind. I need to

get hold of myself. What had I missed, what could I have done? I looked right at the truck, even saw under the trailers.

Where the hell was she?

I see the incident unfold in front of me as if it's a movie I cannot forget. In the back of my mind is the thought, *I know I am not done with this case.*

Chapter 2

The eleven p.m. to seven a.m. graveyard shift continues to be moments of adrenaline rush and hours of routine work, read boredom. Such is the life of a small-town cop. Unless it's a large city, graveyard is pretty much the same anywhere.

In subsequent weeks, the detectives are unable to develop a lead. They find out the lady's name and the fact she was from the next town, ten miles away. She was a secretary for a local business. None of her friends or family had any idea why she would have been in Morgan Hill at that time of night. No one was aware the woman had known a trucker.

The motel has no record of her checking in. It's more of a weekly place, not an overnight stop. The office had closed at seven p.m. the night of her death.

I question the gas station attendant, but he hadn't seen anything. He had probably been asleep. I have found him snoozing on many occasions when patrolling and stopped to check on him. He's one of my nighttime "eyes" when he's awake.

I make it a point to get to know people who work at night: gas station attendants, janitors, city street sweepers, newspaper delivery persons, and especially the all-night diner staff (free coffee is important when working graveyard). I stop in and chat with them, the people who work the same God-awful hours I do. They often have useful information about what's going on in town.

I have worked out a signal with the ones who are the most vulnerable, the ones who have cash on hand. They appreciate this. I drive by slowly and if all looks normal, they wave or keep working. If they scratch their ears, then I know something is wrong. I drive off, then loop back. I leave my car, move up on the building from the side, and peer in the window. What happens next will depend on what I see.

Many times, they are just scratching their ears and do not see me. Their safety depends on the man in the marked police car driving past their windows and they don't look up. Obviously, some people need a refresher course on the "secret signal."

Chapter 3

I have been working for the sheriff's office in the south county for three years now, but my mind is back on the old Morgan Hill case, it never completely goes away. Honestly, it haunts me. I think of it as *my case.* I want to be a detective. Being a detective has always been my goal. The sheriff's office has a promotional exam coming up. There hasn't been an opening for quite a while.

Study time.

I have more than enough time on the job to be eligible to take the test. And I have stayed out of trouble. Being in the south county with limited exposure to supervisors and finger-pointing unhappy citizens, it's been easier than in a high-density area.

Promotional exam, here I come.

The exam for the detective position has now come and gone. I am now in the post-anxiety period. Did I pass? How did I do? Am I in the top five? You must be in the top five to get an interview. We are to be told the result "in a few days."

Going to the briefing each day is fun. Anyone who took the test is looking sideways at the rest of the guys. Does he know? Is he smiling more than usual? Is he grumpier than usual? We are literally driving ourselves nuts.

The results will come in the mail and the top five

candidates will then be scheduled for an interview. More waiting. My mail is delivered while I'm at work, so I must wait until I'm home to find out my results.

****

I get a message from dispatch to call a phone number I don't recognize. I call the number, and it's my bud, Jim. He had gone home to check his mail; he was only five or six miles off his beat. No biggie, he could cover that. I cannot. I'm anywhere from twelve to forty miles from home during my shift.

"I got my notice and I passed in the top five," he yells into the phone.

"I'm happy for you, Jim. Hope you will be happy for me," I yell back.

My results should be at my home, too. I've got six more hours to work. God, do not let there be a big case or accident or anything that holds me over. I *must* get home.

Luckily, I get off on time and rush home for the mail. There it is, my letter from personnel. I take a deep breath, look toward the heavens, and open it.

I passed. I'm in the top five, too. *Yes*. I call Jim. We decide to go out and celebrate. We pay for it the next day, but it was worth it.

Next comes the oral interview. This will be conducted in front of a couple of high-ranking department officials with a representative from Personnel present to make sure it is conducted according to the Personnel Commission rules.

The notice says the top five candidates will be notified of the date and time of the interview. More waiting. It does not say how we will be notified. Are we doing the mail watch thing again or what?

****

The next afternoon I'm on patrol when dispatch directs me to call the office. This is normal and doesn't raise any concern with me. Probably some leftover day shift calls to tidy up. I am close to my former station, so I go use their phone. They still let me come around. After the usual small talk with the guys on duty, I call my office.

My sergeant comes on the line, "Bob, it is with regret I must inform you that your interview is tomorrow at ten hundred hours. Congrats, Bob. I hate to lose you, but you'll make a good detective."

I want to yell, yes, I will be a good detective. Trying not to show emotion, I reply, "Thanks, Sarge, I have enjoyed working with you." After that exchange, I better make it.

The interview is in the sheriff's conference room.

Wow, the prisoners must have backed up the sewer again, so the patrol conference room is not available. The patrol conference room is behind the jail's sewer pipes. Good planning.

After shift, Jim and I get together for a planning session. He has his interview at one p.m. We are both off the next day. We know there are at least two openings, so obviously the two of us are the logical choices.

After some burgers and beer, we get serious. What are we going to wear? This is not a question to be taken lightly. Our future hangs on what the board perceives. Should we wear uniforms or suits? The uniform is easy, but we are off duty. Then again, we are on official business, the interview. A suit will look professional and that's how detectives dress. But will we appear presumptuous or overconfident by wearing the suits?

We're beginning to sound like teenage girls planning what to wear for the prom.

"Does the gun belt make my belly stick out?" I inquire.

"Do the uniform pants accentuate my butt?" Jim jumps from his bar stool, then wiggles and sashays.

"This could go on all night." I laugh. "However, we may not be allowed in here again. People are looking at us."

In the end we go for uniforms, mainly because neither of our suits are exactly fashionable. More like mismatched sport coats and slacks with a wash-and-wear shirt. Oh yeah, ties; I think I have one somewhere. Uniforms it is.

It's a twenty-minute drive to the sheriff's office from my apartment. I leave an hour early for my ten o'clock appointment. Do not want to take any chances.

I pull into the parking lot with plenty of time to spare, so I go into the patrol division's office to grab a cup of coffee. No. Maybe that's not a good idea, I'm nervous enough. I did sleep well, but that was probably because of the beers. I am scrubbed, bright-eyed, and bushytailed. I am ready. So, no coffee. I wander into the squad room and look over the crime reports from last night to kill time. The day shift sergeant sees me. "Hey, Carson, I want to talk to you about the domestic you handled yesterday."

Good, that will take a few minutes and keep my mind off the interview. It turns out the male subject from the domestic dispute has an outstanding felony warrant. I ran him for "wants and warrants" last night, and the results were negative. Someone had misread the printout from the information system. I was told..." the subject has no warrants outstanding."

The office wants to find the guy. I'm the last person to have had contact with him. I had made notes concerning his vehicle and license plate when I sent him packing from his girlfriend's house. But those notes are home. I did not bring my patrol gear and certainly not my notebook. It would have been in my shirt pocket, which would have made my chest look weird.

See how obsessive this fashion thing is?

Sarge wants me to go home and get it—now. I explain why I am here, and I only have twelve minutes left to get upstairs for my interview. He has the gall to ask as if I live across the street. No. I remind him where I'm going. Then he has the poor manners to say, "Doesn't really matter, *they* have already made their choices."

Jerk. I never did like him.

I head upstairs after promising Sarge I'll call him with the info when I get back home.

I step off the elevator and into the inner sanctum of power. Whereas down in patrol you can almost feel the testosterone in the air, up here you feel like you walked into the morgue...stale air, eerie, cold, and quiet. Activity is going on behind closed doors. It does not feel good. Not a comfortable feeling at all.

I walk up to the receptionist, who looks as if she should work in the morgue or possibly be a resident. She's undoubtedly been here since the deputies rode horses. The woman shows me to a sitting area outside the conference room.

"I'll tell them you're here," she informs me in an

ominous tone. Yeah, she lives in the morgue.

At 10:01 the door opens, and the personnel guy emerges. "Deputy Carson, the board is ready for you now."

Inside at a huge, beautiful conference table, the size of a small aircraft carrier, sits *the board*. Immediately I recognize the sheriff, in full uniform. What is he doing here? Sheriffs and chiefs never sit on promotion boards.

I'm introduced to the detective bureau chief resplendent in his green and tan sport coat. *Dug out his best outfit for this.* Then introduced to the sheriff, who says, "Good to see you again."

I stumble over what I hope is an intelligent, coherent answer.

Why is he here? Why does he acknowledge me? Makes it look like we're buds or something. If I get chosen, it will look like favoritism. Oh yeah, Sarge said *they* had already made up their minds. So he can be nice to me, no problem.

Okay, snap out of it. I am here to ace this interview. Settle down and get on with it.

The board is pleasant. They take turns asking questions, typical of most interview boards. The questions are basic—not tricky—common sense. Some are law enforcement oriented, and others are people skills. So far, so good. I feel confident with my answers, maybe too confident. *Stop it. Settle down.*

Okay, I'm better now, again.

When they're finished, they ask the standard last interview question...Do I have any questions? No, I do not. Thank you for your time, etc.

They will notify me of the results in a few days.

More waiting. At least this is the end. Whatever happens now is out of my control.

I walk out past Drusilla. With a happy voice I say, "Have a good day." She seems taken aback with my remark. She smiles a snaggle tooth smile at me.

"Thank you. Same to you."

She may not make it back to the morgue. They may find her at her desk in the morning.

As soon as I get home, I immediately get my notes and call Sarge. He seems somewhat surprised to hear from me. I bet he was ready to jump all over my sergeant about my attitude.

It's eleven thirty a.m. and I call Jim. He's ready to leave for his interview. I promised I would call.

"It was a nightmare. There were six people on the board, and they hammered me the whole time. The sheriff is on the board. I couldn't think straight; it was awful.

"Just kidding; it was tame, in fact, too tame. I expected worse." Now he's going nuts. I level with him, tell him the basics of it, but not questions. I was instructed not to discuss the questions with anyone. He says he will come over when his interview is done. We'll go over the questions and debate our answers until we are crazy.

Chapter 4

It has been three whole days since we took the oral interview and not a peep from anyone. Jim's a basket case while I'm the picture of a calm, composed professional, at peace with the world.

Bullshit, I'm as much a wreck as he is. We both want this to happen, *now*. There are crimes to be solved, our careers to grow, larger paychecks, and all that stuff.

We are led to believe there are two confirmed openings for detective. Three other deputies also took the interview. We know who two of them are but have not learned the name of the third. Is this a conspiracy? Is he/she being kept in the wings? Maybe civil division, jail, or just someone's pet who has been a station monkey and brownnosing their way up. We are not crazy; it's the normal, paranoid thought process during this kind of situation. The fourth day after the interview, I'm out on patrol. I get a dispatch call to meet a K unit at a coffee shop in my beat. K unit is the call sign for the detectives. This is not an unusual occurrence. The detectives often meet with patrol officers to discuss some case we initially handled. I assume it has to do with the guy with the felony warrant from last week.

I pull into the parking lot and see two unmarked units. Are we going to have some action? Often a marked unit is used for their arrests. I quickly go inside.

I see Charlie, a crusty seasoned detective who works the south county and the back of someone's head at a corner booth. Good, we're going to go over a plan. I walk up to them and say hello to Charlie. He's wearing his standard gray sport coat and tan slacks. The other guy looks up. Holy shit, it is the detective bureau chief from the interview. More sedately attired in a dark blue suit. He extends his hand. "How are you doing, Bob? Good to see you again. Have a seat."

I get weak in the knees. Yes, sitting is a good idea. Is this the *thanks for applying but we chose someone else* talk?

Charlie is deadpan. No help from him. The chief, Anthony Woods, breaks into a grin. "Congratulations, Detective, you're our choice, provided you're still interested."

"Oh yes, sir, I most certainly am," I say in the calmest voice I can muster.

Charlie breaks into a laugh and thrusts out his hand. "We are going to have fun."

"I thought you were retiring?" I ask.

"I am but not until the south county is in good hands."

I'm going to die in the damn south county.

Chief Woods tells me to report Monday morning at eight o'clock to the detective bureau. Charlie will be my training officer.

My chest is thumping. I made it.

"Has the other position been filled?" I ask.

The chief says it has; Jim has been chosen. "I told Jim this morning but told him not to say anything until the official announcement is made. Same goes for you."

"Yes, sir."

"By the way, he doesn't know you made it; I know you guys are friends so you can talk to him, but no one else."

"Understood, sir."

After the chief leaves, Charlie immediately removes his tie. We stay for a while. "I'm pleased you were chosen. You know the area, which will be a big help. I told the chief I wanted a south county veteran to replace me."

I am going to die in the south county.

Jim is still on shift, so I wait until I am home to call him. He's cautious on the phone. He doesn't know if I know anything yet, so he's being cagey.

"So how was your day?" I ask calmly.

"Uh...okay, normal, how about you?"

I tell him about some of the routine, dull things that happened. He's getting antsy. We would not normally bother with the norm when talking, especially with the promotion hanging over our heads. I play him a little longer and he's getting uncomfortable.

"Okay, what's going on?" he finally demands. "What's this b.s.?"

"We both saw Chief Woods today, that's all."

"Son of a bitch, I'm dying over this, and you're playing games with me. Jerk."

"Let's go celebrate."

"You're buying, and you're still a jerk."

Chapter 5

My time with Charlie is well spent. He is truly a master of the game. Unassuming in stature and demeanor, no one would suspect he's a cop. His close-cropped gray hair and slight build make him look older than his fifty-something years. Sharp as a tack. He can play dumb questioning suspects and then use their own words to carve up their stories. I sit in awe, in his shadow.

Actually, I sit in the passenger seat. No one drives Charlie. It is *his* black Plymouth. It has seen better days, but the car has been his since he became an investigator. He talks about my being good to "her" when he leaves. I'm not too sure which of them will go first.

I do not think "she" likes me. I have been allowed to drive her places on my own, but I am convinced she feels I am not worthy to be Charlie's replacement. The brakes grab at the most inconvenient moment or the steering wanders in a turn causing me great anxiety. After Charlie retires, I will personally see the She-Devil dies. A detective's job is mostly routine, talking to people who might have seen or heard something, check for any records, and follow up on any possible leads. Sit and have endless cups of coffee with Charlie while discussing the current case and numerous other ones he's handled. This is where the real learning comes in.

The man is a fount of knowledge. It's not wasted time. I absorb all I can from him.

Charlie knows all the players in the south county, as well as everywhere else. If information is needed on some known felon or bad guy who lives in the area, he knows who to ask and get answers. We spend a lot of time talking to people and develop useful information. Is the time spent worth the results? If we didn't spend the time, we would have little or nothing to follow up on to solve a case. This way useful info is obtained. Most of all, thanks to Charlie's way of casually chatting with his people, a lot of non-related information is also obtained. You never know when some offhand comment will provide a clue to another case. Good detectives do this and clear cases while average detectives simply move on to the next case.

I have a case that haunts the back of my mind and I intend to solve it.

Chapter 6

The days fly by. Charlie is retiring by the end of the month; he does not want to, but he knows it's time. Also, there is a wife who insists, in no uncertain terms, it is time. I have progressed acceptably in Charlie's eyes to be his replacement. It has been a good learning experience for me and a lot of fun. I will miss him.

I get to take the lead now and Charlie observes. Afterwards he advises me on what he would have said, done, etc. Best of all, he tells me why his way works or how I *should* have said something. If I am too off-base, he'll step in and take hold of the interview. It's all great learning.

During one of our informative coffee breaks, I decide to ask Charlie about "my case," when I may have witnessed the woman being dragged to death by the truck.

Charlie remembers hearing about it. He listens while I tell him how it has bothered me, and I want to see it solved.

He puts down his coffee. "You're a detective now, correct?"

"Uhh, yeah."

"Well detective, why don't you begin by going to the involved agencies and ask to see their files on the case?"

"But I don't have any cases like that."

He informs me it is not unusual for one jurisdiction to look at similar cases in other areas.

"Dig." He slams his cup down on the table. "Haven't I taught you anything?"

Okay, I feel like the karate kid now.

"You can follow up on anything you feel is a possible lead. We have enough open cases in this county you can go almost anywhere on a follow-up. If you're actively working cases, no one is going to question you. But keep on top of the current ones. The brass will want to know about them occasionally."

Properly chastised, I go to Morgan Hill P.D. and ask to check their files. Nothing I didn't already know, but that's good. My baseline is still as I remembered it. A few days later I visit the CHP office in San Jose to check on a parallel incident. They have done a little work on the case but left it pending, as no leads were developed.

Okay, so there is nothing new for me to look at. But as Charlie reminded me, I am a detective now. I can follow this where I want. What has not been done? Who has not been interviewed? My mentor before Charlie was Tony from Morgan Hill P.D. He always maintained, "Somebody knows. *Someone* has seen *something*. You just have to find that person."

Tony is always chatting with anyone and everyone during his shift and off duty. Charlie does the same. These two are collecting information and filing it away. Like the computers of today, they compile their information, search their hard drive (brain), and put two and two together.

Ah, Grasshopper, you are beginning to come awake, I hear in my head. *Mayagi has hope for you.*

Along with my current cases I begin to build a file on what is known about "my case." My file goes with me everywhere and when I have the opportunity, I continually look for information to add.

I come in one morning and Charlie hands me a set of car keys. Charlie's due for a new car. Lord knows the She-Devil has been overdue for replacement. He simply refused to take one. As a parting gesture he has agreed to take a new car and turn it over to his replacement, if he could keep the Plymouth for his last few days.

I now get *my own car*. Yes, the She-Devil will be retired along with Charlie. *There is a God.* I get a new Dodge. It was to be Charlie's, so I lucked out. It is gray. Not black or white, but gray. We haven't formed a relationship yet, but I think "he" likes me.

I need to shake it down, so with Charlie's approval, I am going to visit the crime scenes comparable to "my case" and see what I can dig up.

There has been a similar case recently, beside the freeway in San Jose. Being so close in proximity to "my case" I want to find out everything I can.

Arriving, I see alongside the highway is an old, sagging chain link fence. Beyond the boundary is a trucking company's terminal. The company uses the area near the highway for parking their empty trailers. The terminal buildings are on the far side of the lot, away from the fence.

I drive to the terminal office and meet the manager, a nicely dressed petite woman in her forties. Does not seem like the right fit. About then a burly driver comes into the office whining about something. She immediately puts him in his place and sends him out the door, tail between his legs. Okay, so much for typecasting.

"I'm here to investigate a women's body found outside the perimeter of your trucking yard."

"I know about the incident on the freeway; in fact, one of my yardmen was working that night. He told me about it."

"When does he comes to work next?"

"Today, at midnight."

"I need to talk to him." She offers to call him, but I want to interview him at night, under the same circumstances, to get a clear idea of what he may or may not have seen. Besides, it is ten a.m.; if he works graveyard, he's barely getting to sleep. I don't want him cranky.

It is set; I will arrive at midnight and meet with Otto.

Back at the office Charlie is proud of me. "Now you're thinking like a detective."

At midnight I go to the trucking company and meet with Otto, a solid looking man in his fifties. "I was a truck driver but now, no more long hauls. My job is to keep the terminal open at night for incoming and outgoing trucks. I also move the trailers around as needed."

"What about on the night of the incident on the freeway?" I probe like a friend, just interested in his story.

"I was backing an empty trailer up to the freeway fence. There were a bunch of police cars and an ambulance out there."

I stop him. "Did you see a truck parked on the shoulder *before* the emergency vehicles arrived?"

"I did see a truck parked on the shoulder of the freeway. It was right before the police came. I didn't put the two incidents together as being connected. Accidents always happen out there. Sorry, I don't pay much attention to the news, except for sports. I just went to get another trailer and as I was parking it, I noticed the truck still there. I went over to the fence to see if there was a problem. The truck was about seventy-five feet down the roadway from me and facing my way. The headlights were on so I couldn't see much behind them, but heard the slamming of a door, then saw the driver walk in front of the truck's headlights toward the shoulder side. I couldn't get any closer. My yard don't go that far down the freeway."

He tells me he finished parking his trailer and looked down the freeway toward the truck. He saw the driver pass again in front of the headlights, walking back toward the driver's side. Then the truck pulled away.

We go out into the yard, and Otto shows me where he was and where the truck was located. With the dark highway and headlights of the truck on, he could not have seen past the front of the truck. When it pulled out it would still be in the dark as it passed Otto.

"What can you remember about the truck, Otto?"

"All I can recall is that it was a conventional sleeper cab, dark colored, pulling an enclosed trailer."

Before I can ask, Otto tells me he could read the name of the trucking company on the trailer: Brown Freight.

Finally, I have a real clue. No one had talked to Otto or the trucking company.

"I'd been busy in the terminal office after parking

the last trailer and wasn't directly aware of the police and ambulance. I went out onto the loading dock to smoke and saw the flashing lights on the shoulder of the freeway. Don't tell the manager I was smoking; she forbids it on the premises."

"I promise."

Back at the office I am proud of myself as I tell Charlie what I learned. In typical fashion he calmly says, "so have you found the Brown Freight company yet?"

"I just got back."

"What are you waiting for? Clues get cold, and they can be out of business by the time you get around to it."

Slinking off to my desk I start my search for the company.

Chapter 7

This is Charlie's last day. Tomorrow is his retirement party, which should be quite an affair. Friends and enemies from over the years will be there.

Today he is out saying his good-byes. He wants to go on his own and I agree. Yesterday I found the Brown Freight Line. Lucky for me they're still in business. They are located in Stockton, about a two-hour drive from San Jose. The terminal manager is expecting me.

About ten-thirty a.m. I arrive. The manager is more like you would expect, fifties, overweight, and balding. He is harried, disheveled, and constantly looking out the window to see what the crew is doing. Or maybe he is waiting for the bill collectors to close them down. The place looks that way. Not kept up, a mess...literally.

I ask, "Who could have been driving in San Jose on the night in question?"

He rummages through stacks of drivers' logs, schedules, and who knows what else. After going to a back room, he eventually emerges with a schedule of a run from Salinas to Sacramento on the day in question. There is one where the time frame fits. He goes looking for the driver's log. Again, he disappears into the abyss. He emerges several minutes later.

"I got the name for ya. Bill Weaton."

The driver's logbook shows Weaton made the

delivery in Sacramento at seven a.m. the morning of the incident. Time enough to leave the crime scene and get to his delivery.

I, of course, ask the obvious, "Is he still employed?"

Of course, he is not. It's not going to be that easy.

"He was a typical on-the-spot hire, license was current, and DMV record acceptable. His Kenworth tractor was in good condition. It's dark blue in color with no striping or other decoration. You know, just one of the thousands of Kenworths out on the road."

"Did he leave his truck?" I inquire. Of course not. He drove away in it.

"Mr. Weaton quit when he finished that run. Didn't say why or where he was going. Took his final check and I ain't seen him since. No forwarding address. But I can give you his local address. The one he gave the company when he was hired."

The address is a post office box in Modesto, a few miles down the highway.

No one at Brown Freight can tell me much about Weaton. He only worked for two months. Seemed to be a loner, they said. But I get his driver's license and vehicle registration information from their records. Clues are building up in my file.

I go to Modesto and manage to get the postmaster to check out his mailbox. Stuffed full of junk mail, except for a letter mailed two weeks ago from Oklahoma. It is from a G. Weaton. I want that letter.

The postmaster informs me in his professional voice, "Of course, I can't give it to you, but the box rental is due and will be closed for non-payment. The letter will be returned to the sender."

I had already told the postmaster why I wanted to locate Weaton. I even offer to hand carry it to the addressee. The postmaster says he cannot allow that. Then I get a flash. I know a postal inspector in San Jose I helped out of a jam. I ask the postmaster if I can call the inspector, as he is working with me on this case. Technically not true, but he hands me to a phone, and I call Steve, who luckily, is in the office. I immediately explain what I'm doing. He has me give the phone to the postmaster. The next thing I know, I am signing a release for the letter. *Thank you, Steve.*

I cannot decide if I should rip open the letter or try to steam it open to be more subtle. I decide on the latter and head back to the San Jose office. We have lab people who can open it with no detection whatsoever.

As I'm approaching San Jose, Charlie calls me on the radio. "Where are you?"

"I'm about ten minutes from the station."

"Hurry up; I need your help."

I'm not too worried. He probably has all sorts of gifts and mementos he collected today and needs help getting them into the office.

A few minutes later he calls again, asking how much longer. I tell him I'm around the corner.

"Hurry it up; don't stop for coffee," says the coffee hound. Boy, he is cranky.

Pulling into our lot I do not see the She-Devil in his parking place.

"Where are you? I'm at your spot."

"I'm in the back where you park. Get over here." He is getting pissed.

I swing around and go to the back of the parking lot. There in my spot is the She-Devil angled up against another investigator's car. How did he do that?

I go up to him. He's behind the wheel, sweating like a pig. I reach for the door handle and pull on it. Nothing happens. He yells for me to get him out. I have to say the obvious; "Pull on the handle," and I point inside.

"I did that, you fool. It broke."

He holds up the interior door handle. Yep, it's broken. I look at the right side of his car. It is wedged up against the other car. I know Charlie has the rear doors locked, so they can't be opened from the inside. You never know who you will have back there. But they don't work from the outside either. What the hell? The driver's window is up because it came off the track some time ago. Charlie is trapped. I knew it. Final run and she is not going to let him go. I start to laugh.

"It's not funny; get me out of here," he yells. "I'm dying of the heat and I have to pee."

I can't resist. "Shouldn't drink so much coffee."

By now we have drawn a crowd of detectives and uniforms. Everyone must look and then laugh. Charlie's ready to shoot us all.

I take charge of the delicate situation. I tell Charlie to put the car in neutral and we will all push him away from the other car so he can crawl out the side. Good plan…Wrong. The power steering has let go. That is the reason he could not steer in the first place and ended up snuggled so tight against the car next to him. He can't turn the wheel enough for us to get him off the other car.

Finally, we get him to climb over to the passenger window, which still works, as two of us stand on the cars and pull him out.

Without even a "thanks" he runs off to pee.
We beat the She-Devil.

Chapter 8

The retirement party goes as expected. A grand time is had by most, some don't remember it, and Charlie is well-behaved. He is somewhat overwhelmed by the turnout. He takes me aside and tells me if I need any help with a case to feel free to call him. I tell him I appreciate his offer and his ideas will always be welcome.

"Ideas, hell!" he snorted. "If you need me to go talk to one of those assholes, I'll be glad to do it. Can't waste thirty-five years of police work."

Charlie definitely does not want to retire. I will be calling on him, but as for him "talking to the assholes" I'm not so sure, but then again he's good with them.

Now back to work. My case assignments are typical: burglaries, gas station robberies, miscellaneous theft reports. Nothing exciting. At least no bank robberies. Those are never fun. You must share any information you obtain with the FBI and they do not share s—t with you. Still, we must take the time to attempt to work the case. It should be ours or theirs, not both. That is my opinion *and* the opinion of most local law enforcement personnel. Since most bank robbers do not stop at only one job and they move around jurisdictions, the FBI is the logical agency to handle each case. So why do we even bother?

I'm working on getting all the information I can on

William Randall Weaton, the full name of my murder suspect. He's Caucasian, five-eleven, one hundred and seventy-five pounds, blue eyes and blond hair. This is all off the copy of his Georgia driver's license I obtained from Brown Freight. Registration on the Kenworth truck shows the legal owner is a finance company in Georgia. His driver's license is due to expire in less than two months.

The national commercial driver's license program has not yet become law. When it does, it will allow the tracking of anyone who drives a commercial vehicle anywhere in the country. At this point of my investigation, I can only run his name and social security number through the national criminal data base, an ancient teletype system developed before computers.

My boy Bill did have a few traffic citations in various states, mostly related to trucking, speeding, weight violations, and that type of thing. Nothing recent, so no addresses to follow up on.

I place an APB (All Points Bulletin) out on the national network. This has the truck information, license number, and William Weaton's ID facts. I am to be notified if he or the truck is located. This is almost a needle in the haystack. The truck's a common color, has no name on it, and if it is pulling a trailer, no one will see the license plate. If Mr. Weaton gets stopped, it will depend on whatever the police agency's procedures are, whether they check the national database or not.

I contact the Georgia finance company who holds the title to the truck. Weaton's behind on payments; surprise, surprise. They would very much like to find him, too. We agree to share any information we may develop. The truck was sold to him in Georgia from a used truck dealer. The residential address was a weekly motel. According to the finance company, he had a job but has since moved on.

I get a feeling about Georgia. Further checking turns up some old traffic citations from many years ago. Not trucking stuff; speeding, reckless, and one accident, all in passenger vehicles. I request addresses from the records section of the Georgia Department of Motor Vehicles. Dealing with the friendly southern records staff is a slow, but eventually productive, process. I develop a relationship with a records supervisor named Brenda. Since she doesn't have much going on now, she takes an interest in my quest. Georgia boy gone wrong; she does not like that. She is going to dig for me.

Now I better spend some time on my current cases. I, in fact, have a cattle rustling situation. Ah, shades of the old west. Well, this is the modern west; someone drove a cattle truck right up to a rancher's field and loaded up his herd. Of course, no witnesses, only a few tire tracks from the hauler and a lot of hoof prints.

The rancher tells me, "I had rounded up my herd for shipment to market only the day before and was waiting for the hauler I'd hired. At first, the herd was to be picked up the next day, but the hauler called me and said he was stuck out of town and would not be back for at least two days. Some damn thief beat him to it."

"I assume you checked with the hauler to see if he came early?"

"I called the morning I discovered the cattle were gone. He wasn't there, but his wife said she would have him call me. I asked if he picked up my herd last night.

She said he'd been in Fresno at the livestock auction for two days."

"Did he call you?"

"Yes, that night he called and said he was in Fresno and had not been over here since I last saw him."

I go to nearby ranches and ask if anyone noticed anything unusual. Nothing. I remember Tony's slogan...*Someone* has seen *something*. You just need to find them.

The next day driving in the area I see an irrigator in a field across from the scene of the cattle rustling. This is a farm hand who works the ditches that supply water to the fields. The irrigators are all over an area. Digging open a channel and plugging up another. It is their responsibility to stop a field from becoming over-flooded. So they are out at all hours.

I park and find a gate to the field. Don't want to tear my good detective clothes on barbed wire. I go up to the worker. He is, as usual, a seasonal hire. Summer jobs between classes.

"Yes, I indeed saw the truck take the cattle. It was at dusk and I was working my ditches across the road. There were two white guys, wearing cheap straw cowboy hats. I couldn't really see their faces. They had their hats yanked down, just above their eyes. They pulled the truck up to the corral and herded the cattle up the ramps into the trailer, then drove off."

Pretty much what I expected. But I hit the jackpot when I ask if he can remember anything about the truck. The talented young teenager is apparently an aspiring truck driver. He tells me the make, model, color, and even the name on the door of truck. He wrote it in the dirt in the field: G. Howell & Sons.

The truck was white, and the name was written in black letters. He did not recognize the name or the company. Had not seen them before, but he wasn't suspicious because the cattle were obviously penned up for shipping.

After profusely thanking him, I leave my star witness. Man, I hope the next time something happens in this area, that kid is around. Best witness I have ever found. Shoveling dirt...waste of talent.

I talk with the victim rancher and ask if he has heard of the company.

"I've heard of the Howell outfit, but I haven't used them. I think they're from Hollister, a small town in San Benito County, about an hour away."

I go into the Gilroy Police Department and use their phone to call the San Benito Sheriff's Office. I talk with Dennis, the investigator for the department. He says he knows the Howells. Old man is okay, but the kids are trouble. We arrange to meet the next day and check out the Howells.

At ten a.m., I meet Dennis at a coffee shop. He's hungry and wants breakfast. Sounds good to me. Dennis tells me, "I've done some checking. Dad Howell is getting too old to drive much and the boys are handling the day-to-day business." He points at me with his toast, using it to emphasize his thoughts. "Those damn boys have been in numerous bar fights and other alcohol-related trouble for years. I 'happened' to run into Dad Howell yesterday and found out the boys just got back from delivering a load of cattle. Dad didn't know where they went but said they 'done good;' came home with a lot of money."

Finishing my coffee, I relate my thoughts to

Dennis. "The problem now is finding out who they sold the herd to. Since the cattle were branded, the buyer was not legit. It could be another rancher who would try to change the brand or an illegal meat packer."

Dennis is going to keep snooping on his end, and I head back to my county.

On a whim, I stop by the victim's ranch again and ask who he hired to take the herd.

He says, "It was Bull Haulers Inc., a new company who offered me an 'introductory price' well below the norm. The owner, Billy Boyd, came and signed the deal. Billy's company was going to pick up the herd late at night. Billy asked for the papers and the money, so I wouldn't have to stay up late."

I might be a novice at this cattle business, but the victim is not. "Why would you do this?" I inquire. The rancher says it isn't unusual for a trucker to pick up at a late hour on their way back from another run. Yes, usually the rancher would be present, but since this was going to be anywhere between two and four a.m., he went along with it.

The picture's getting clearer. With the paperwork Billy Boyd picked up from the victim, the cattle were legal game to sell. I ask for a phone number or any address for Boyd and Bull Haulers Inc. The rancher produces a handwritten receipt for the money he paid Billy to haul the load.

Billy told the rancher he was just starting out in business, so his printed receipts hadn't arrived yet.

The rancher's beginning to follow my drift. *Yes, sir ...you may have been taken.*

"Have you heard from Billy?" I ask. "What about the money you gave him?"

"He said he would drop it by on Friday when he got home from Fresno. He was real nice about it. Said it was terrible somebody would steal another's livestock."

Guess who is going to be waiting for Billy on Friday at the ranch?

Chapter 9

This is getting fun now. I'm sinking my teeth into my first big case. I must methodically get the details down and check everything. Charlie's rules.

Was there a cattle auction in Fresno this week? Well, I find out there is a cattle auction somewhere in the area every week. Okay, so now, did my suspects attend one and did they sell cattle? The answer to that question is not so easy. I call the Fresno County S.O. and talk with a detective.

He gives me to their "cattle man," Sgt. Kramer. Kramer is the next voice I hear. Only he is a she. Sergeant Kathy Kramer is the department's expert in livestock crimes.

Sergeant Kathy knows her game. She will check with her people and get back to me. By *people,* she is referring to the auction houses, ranchers, and other sources she has developed over the years. I don't know how old she is, but on the phone she's noteworthy. I want to meet her.

I get a call from Brenda in Georgia. I've got women everywhere, but no dates yet. Maybe it's time to start thinking about a social life beyond drinking with my buds.

Back to Brenda in Georgia. She has developed a small case file on the suspicious long-haul trucker. She traced his address history from motor vehicle records, arrest reports, and whatever else she could dig up. She has an address that appears to be a parents' residence or at least where he lived when he began to "enter the system." First arrest, traffic tickets, etc. She says the address is several years old, but "folks don't move around much here. So I bet the parents are still at this address, if they're alive." She is going to check further with the county property and tax records office and let me know if the folks are still living there.

I thank her abundantly. She says with a southern drawl, "If this works out, are y'all coming out here?" Sounds like a pickup line to me.

"Sure will." Hell, I'm getting more action from my office than in any bar.

Tomorrow is Friday when Billy Boyd, of Bull Haulers, is to meet with the rancher and give him back his check. The time is set for around noon. I check with the victim who has heard nothing further.

Sergeant Kathy calls from Fresno County Sheriff's Office. No leads so far, but she will keep checking. While we're talking, she mentions having to leave early and go to her grandkid's graduation. Well, that takes her out of the equation.

I need more information on the Howell boys. I call Dennis in the San Benito S.O. to see if he has anything further for me.

"I was about to call you," Dennis says. "The Howell boys were not in Fresno this week. They got a speeding ticket coming up from Salinas yesterday. I happened to run into a highway patrol guy I know at coffee.

"Anyway, the CHP asked about the boys because he thought they were acting awfully nervous when he pulled them over. He found nothing wrong; they even let him search the truck. Nothing of interest; a lot of cow dung in the trailer and a few empty beer cans in the truck. They told him they had just come from an auction in King City. He gave them a ticket for speeding and sent them on their way."

This is great news. King City is nowhere near Fresno. The boys are lying to the victim. One of them must be "Billy Boyd" of Bull Haulers, or at least they are accomplices. Dennis has the booking photos of the boys from their last stay in the "county hotel."

Formally, they are Robert and James Howell. Locally they're known as Bobby and Jimmy. Dennis is willing to meet me tomorrow at the victim's ranch with the photos. He's thinking this is not the boys' first caper. There have been similar cases in his county but no terrific witness like I found. Back at work with the descriptions of the Howells, I gather a few photos from our mug shot file. To be legal I need to have several pictures of similar appearing males to show any witnesses.

It's a pleasant Friday morning as I head south to the victim's ranch. I can't help thinking, *this is a good day to arrest someone.*

Dennis and I meet up at a Gilroy coffee shop for breakfast…I mean to compare notes and plan our strategy.

Their photos look like the victim's description of Billy Boyd. Thirty to forty years of age, average height, and shaggy hair; describes most of the white males in the area. What I want on the way to the ranch is to find my witness and show him the photos.

Luckily, I spot my guy out standing in his field.

He cannot ID the boys; it was almost dark when he saw the incident. Also, he repeats the fact they were wearing straw cowboy hats. Man, what a good witness; not much escapes him.

Dennis and I go to the ranch and the rancher lets us park in the barn, so we won't tip off Billy. While we're waiting, his wife serves us coffee and homemade cookies. We are full from our strategy meeting, but can't be impolite, can we?

We show him the array of photos and he goes right to Jimmy Howell.

"That's Billy," he says with no hesitation.

Noon comes and goes; it is approaching one p.m. We have each made a couple of trips to the bathroom and cannot drink any more coffee.

Then our host, who has been sitting at the window, says, "Here he comes."

Sure enough, here comes a pickup truck barreling up the dirt driveway. Two males are inside. I step into the dining room and Dennis crams himself into the tiny hall closet by the front door. He lost the coin toss. We send the Mrs. upstairs.

The rancher opens the door and invites the boys in. Immediately Billy hands over the rancher's check and begins to tell him again how terrible it is someone would steal another's livestock.

I had instructed the rancher that once he got the check in his hand, he was to move away from the door like he was going to put it away.

"It's against the Bible," good ol' Billy says seriously. "Thou shalt not steal."

"Yeah, and God's going to get you for that." I step

out of the dining room, and Dennis explodes out of the closet.

Bobby and Jimmy are dumbfounded and crash into each other trying to get to the door. Dennis is there and the two of us get them in cuffs without further ado.

By the time they stop crying, wailing, and blaming each other, I do not have much to do except read them their rights. Between the two of them, they pretty much confess to the cattle rustling, a gas theft, drinking while driving, and about half of the penal code.

Dennis and I load one in each of our cars and take them to the Gilroy P.D. to book them. By the time Dennis gets Jimmy to Gilroy, he has confessed to three or four other cattle rustlings. Bobby's not as talkative with me. He only admits to one other job.

After we finish booking them, we're laughing our asses off.

"Boy, you raise 'em smart down there," I say.

"The smart ones leave; this is what's left."

We both have an hour to drive back to our offices, so we can't have a celebratory drink. We promise to get together again.

As a parting shot Dennis says, "Next time you need to clean up a case in your county, call me."

Chapter 10

Bobby and Jimmy Howell have their day in court. It doesn't take long. Each has his own public defender, who appears embarrassed to be there. The boys are a mess. Right down to the end they point fingers at each other. It's the feeblest attempt at making a defense I have ever seen. The judge quickly passes sentence and orders them to be transferred to San Benito County for trial on the several charges Dennis and the county attorney had filed.

Dennis testifies for my case, and I will have to do the same for him. With any justice, they'll be locked up until they are at least twice as old as Dad Howell. Speaking of Dad, he is present in court but does not speak to the boys. He is plainly disgusted with them.

I go back to the office after court. Entering the office, I see a man in his thirties talking with the boss's secretary. He is dressed in a dark suit, hair trimmed neatly and clean shaven.

FBI; who else?

When Sarah spots me, she points at me. Great, whose rights did I violate recently? I mean why else would he be here. *They* do not need *our* help; we just get in the way. With no other choice, I go over to them.

"Bob, this is Special Agent Mazzaro of the FBI. He would like to talk to you," she gushes.

Sarah, Sarah, Sarah, as long as you have been

here you still hold them in awe?

"Glad to meet you, Agent Mazzaro." I extend my hand.

"Andy." He gives me a real man's handshake. Not the usual pathetic, formal *must-I-touch-the-unworthy* type you usually get.

Andy wants to discuss cattle rustling and specifically my recent case. Seems he covers an area that includes the federal land in Monterey County. Some dastardly persons have stolen cattle from government land. He heard about my case from the newspapers and wanted to check out leads.

Hey, sure, why not; he seems to be human. Good handshake, used the first name. He must be new.

It turns out he is not new and is a good guy. How'd he slip through?

I fill him in on my case but tell him Dennis will probably have more by now that might help. I only have one case; Dennis has three or four. I'm not sure how many the Howell boys finally confessed to.

"Yes, but you have the perps in your jail now. I'd like to talk to them. Tomorrow morning, they're going to be transferred to San Benito to be tried on those cases."

He looks almost conspiratorial.

"If I could talk to them before they get to their home turf, I might be able to get more out of them."

He is asking me for a favor. I'm basically done with this case. The FBI wants me to help. This could pay off in the future, provided the FBI doesn't catch on to the fact Andy is a real person, not a federal machine.

I call the jail lieutenant, an old bud from patrol days. This is a little out of the norm. No attorneys present. I explain to the lieutenant they've already been mirandized and convicted. I just need to clear up some loose ends so I can close my case, I lie. I also forget to mention Andy.

We meet with Jimmy first. Andy's smooth. Tells him he needs help with some cases in the southern Monterey area and maybe Jimmy can assist.

"I ain't ever been in Monterey."

"Not the city, Jimmy," I say. "Monterey County, like King City."

"Oh yeah. What do you want to know? We already told you guys about all we did."

Andy works him beautifully. "Since you know the area, you know some of the people there, maybe you overheard them talking, something that could help me with my case. You know, I could talk to the District Attorney in San Benito and maybe get you a lighter sentence."

Andy throws out a few things and, in a while, Jimmy has given up three of his associates.

"But Bobby and me didn't have nothing to do with any of those things."

Next, we try Bobby. He is more cautious but eventually comes around to basically the same group Jimmy told us about.

As Andy and I are leaving the jail he says, "Hey, it's dinner time. Let's go grab a bite."

This is not right. What universe am I in? The FBI does not invite you to have coffee, let alone a meal. If you are in their office, they will refrain from drinking their coffee while you are present. Must be in their procedural manual.

Andy and I have a good time. Go to a grill, have a

few beers and burgers, laugh, talk, and tell lies. Good time. He lives in Morgan Hill, recently transferred from the San Francisco area. He covers mostly rural areas as I do, but a much greater size. Andy tells me to stop by his office or even his home if I'm down there on the weekends. Personally, I think it's a trap, but we agree to help each other whenever possible.

Chapter 11

A few weeks later as I'm leaving the office, I get a call from Brenda, the Georgia records lady who is helping me find my trucker suspect.

In her soft southern drawl, she says, "I had one of the deputies I know, such a sweet gentleman he is, go by that address from the time back when that Weaton boy was arrested?"

She is making a statement sound like a question, but that's how she talks.

"Anyway, I was right. His folks still live there. They haven't heard from him in a couple of months. Bubba, that's the deputy's name, I know other folks think everyone is named Bubba in the South, but he really is Bubba. Anyway, Bubba said he was checking on references for a county job, and someone had given their boy's name as a character reference. Bubba is so clever."

I thank Brenda and get the parents' information.

"Y'all thinking of coming down soon?" asks her soft syrupy voice.

"Not yet, but it's getting closer," I reply with my most sincere manly tone.

Taking stock of my new role as a detective, things are looking rather good. I have two cattle rustlers convicted and my boss is elated. I am building my Bill Weaton suspicious trucker case. But I haven't located him...yet.

Charlie would say sit down with all your facts and read them as if it were the first time you've seen them. Keep your mind open and forget any foregone conclusions. So on the way out the door I grab my file. Tonight, I sit down with Bill Weaton and Coors.

In my file is a note about the letter he had in his P.O. box. I have been busy, but how could I have forgotten about it? No excuse; who's a detective now, dammit.

I make a plan. Tomorrow I will call Steve, the postal inspector, and hope he's in the mood to do me another favor. I need a name and address for the box holder. Then I'll go to our crime lab and visit the harried, overworked staff who unfortunately owe me nothing. Humm...one male and two females; donuts, perfect.

Next morning, I stop by the donut shop and get a dozen, half chocolate and half glazed. Should be enough, but I need to sneak in without going through the detective bureau or I'll be mobbed. The cops-and-donut thing is not a joke.

I am a hit with the lab. The ladies are thrilled, and the lone male hasn't come in yet. Perfect, I deal better with them. In a few minutes they hand me the envelope and letter. Like it was never touched. I thank them gratefully and promise more donuts.

Steve, the postal inspector, isn't in when I call so I leave the hated voice mail message...call me. *Please.*

Now to the letter. I feel I should hide somewhere when I open it. It might be technically incorrect to read it, but a postal inspector let me have it, so here goes.

The return address on the envelope says only G.

Weaton. On the inside is a handwritten letter on binder paper. It appears to be written with emotion as the pen almost cuts through the paper. The outside handwriting, I think is female. Pretty sure I'm right as it is signed, "No longer your Bitch!"

The note begins, "Asshole" and then goes on to advise him she will "cut off his dick" if he ever steps foot in Oklahoma again. Not a love letter. She says she knows about the whore he dumped out of his truck at the hospital. "She died, you bastard; you killed her. I know you did. You ever come around me again and I'll tell the police what I know."

Good I got the letter before Bill Weaton did. This woman is asking to be silenced.

When the postal inspector calls me back, I relay the details of my case to him. Since a threat was made through the United States mail, he can formally help me. He will get me all the information he can find on the owner of the P.O. box. I need the address of G. Weaton. She needs to talk to a police officer, soon.

Now I go to my mentor, Charlie. I need his input on how to proceed. I have what I consider are enough facts to ask the Enid, Oklahoma Police Department for a follow up.

Charlie yells, "Hell no. You go to Enid and do your own investigating. It's your case."

"Can I do that?" I detect a whine in my voice.

"You tell Chief of Detectives Bradbury you can tie this guy into two homicides in our county and the one in Oklahoma."

"Uh, I only have the one homicide here, Charlie."

"Don't forget your personal case from Morgan Hill."

"Charlie, I don't have any facts or evidence on that."

He gives a disgruntled sigh. "Son, you were a witness, the circumstantial facts on that case match the others. Maybe not enough to prove in court, but you can't say it wasn't him, can you?"

"No, but I want to be able to prove who did that one and I can't yet."

"That is why *you*"—he points his finger at me, which he seems to do often—-"need to go to Oklahoma. You don't want some Barney Fife in Oklahoma messing up your only good lead."

Charlie continues to give me more tips on how to approach Chief Bradbury. "Just subtly indicate solving our cases, as well as one in Oklahoma, would look good for our county. Which means it would make Bradbury look good with the sheriff. Bradbury will seize on the idea. The detective bureau hasn't made any good headlines lately." Charley gives me a look which makes me feel I should go stand in the corner for a while.

Now the pressure's on me. If I don't come through, then I will die in the south county. I'm beginning to think I will anyway. What the hell, I'm going for it. I want a crack at this.

Next day I head over to set up an appointment with Chief Bradbury. This is how Charlie said to do it. Do not walk in expecting to get his undivided attention. Make him set aside some time for you.

I stop by Bradbury's office and talk with Sarah. She seems to have come back down to earth after having met the "FBI." Unbeknownst to me, the chief is in his office with the door open and can hear me as I ask for an appointment. He yells out, "Come on in,

Bob, what can I do for you?"

Oh crap. I have nothing with me, I need to prepare, have my ducks in a row, all that stuff. Well, no choice. I go in.

"Good to see you, Bob," he says holding out his hand. "Great job on the cattle rustling. Loved it; so did the sheriff."

I shake his hand firmly. What an opening for me.

I tell the chief about my case. I quickly outline the whole picture, then give him the solid facts and sort of ease the rest of them in at the same time. He sits back in his chair and is quiet. I don't know if he is going to laugh at me or throw me out. I am unable to read his face, I'm holding my breath. He sits forward, looks straight at me, and in a deep, strong voice says, "Sarah, get this man reservations to Enid, Oklahoma. He's got a hot case to solve."

Then to me, "Go get that son of a gun, Detective."

Charlie, you are a genius.

Chapter 12

I can't wait to call Charlie.

He is very calm. "Didn't I tell you it would work?"

"Yeah, sure; why did I doubt you, Mr. Mayagi?"

"Who? Is that the strawberry farmer?"

"Never mind."

Steve, the postal inspector has gotten me the name and address of the box holder in Enid.

It is...wait for it...William Weaton. Street address appears to be an apartment, unit 210.

My travel is arranged. I call the Enid Police Department and speak to the head of detectives. He is professional, not at all a "Barney Fife." He'll have a detective pick me up at the airport and even recommends a hotel. "Nice place, not too pricey. Good bar."

Pinch me. What happened to the inter-agency rivalry, backstabbing, we-solve-our-own-cases type mentality? Or is that just with the FBI?

I arrive in Enid as scheduled and sure enough, there to meet me is Detective Gregory. He is not named Barney. Nice guy about my age, single. Dressed in sport coat, slacks, with open neck. No tie. We hit it off right away. We go to his office and I show him my case file.

"That's Gloria, from the hospital emergency room," he says as he goes over the letter. "Man, she sounds furious. I haven't spoken to her often, but she doesn't talk like that."

He is shocked by the harsh language in the letter. "Gloria's an admitting clerk; the local cops know her and the rest of the ER staff. All good people."

We decide to drive by her address to become familiar with the area. I suggest we check the file on the "whore" mentioned in the letter, and see what information is available on her. Greg was not involved in that case and knows nothing about it.

At the Enid, Oklahoma PD station I meet the head of detectives and some of the other detectives. I feel like I am from Hollywood or someplace. I'm asked all kinds of questions about our equipment, weapons, labs, etc. The California image is way overblown here.

I like that.

The woman from the hospital has a name and probably was a prostitute. She was known by the local police to hang out at the nearby truck stop on the interstate. She had a minor criminal record, nothing major.

Some of the detectives know Gloria a little from the hospital and say she has a husband who is a long-haul trucker. No one has met him or knows his name. When they check the information I give them on William Weaton, it is a different story. William has a record of public drunkenness, disturbing the peace, and domestic violence. The domestics do not involve Gloria. There are three complaints from different women in the area. All the women had called the police saying he hit them. But after the police arrived and got William out, the women did not want to press charges.

Now it is time to see Gloria Weaton. She works

swing shift at the emergency room, so we decide to wait and see her at home rather than at her workplace. We'll go by first thing in the morning. It is now after four p.m. and I need to check into my hotel. Greg suggests we have dinner and drinks after. Good idea.

A couple of the other detectives stop by and we make a night of it. These boys know how to drink.

At eight a.m. next morning, Greg is knocking at my door, "Ready to go, city boy?" He seems bright-eyed and bushy-tailed; me, I'm a little hung over.

We go to the station and when we walk in, one of the guys we were drinking with last night yells out, "Hey you two, come over here."

He is looking at last night's patrol log. "Turns out Bill Weaton made a visit to Gloria last night about two in the morning. According to the responding officers' report, she would not open the door and when he tried to kick it open, she fired a couple of rounds through the door. Bill was nowhere to be seen by the time the officers arrived. They told her to keep the door locked and call them if he returned."

There was no mention of my interest in Weaton.

Greg and I go to Gloria's apartment. Sure enough, there are two bullet holes in the door. If he had been directly in front of the door he would have been hit. No blood stains on the porch. Shame; would have been nice.

We knock and immediately Greg calls out, "Police Department." We do not want a similar response if she thinks Weaton is back. We both stand to the side of the doorway, standard procedure when unsure of the occupants' response to the police. But then you are never sure what the response to *Police* will be.

Gloria opens the door. She looks like hell. In her thirties, auburn hair is a mess, no makeup, still in a bathrobe. Not a good night for her. She asks us in, and we talk about last night. Gloria says she did not want him around and had told him so. She didn't see how he left; only heard him run down the apartment stairs. She heard no vehicle.

"How did you tell him you didn't want to see him anymore?" I ask.

"I sent him a letter. He's working in California because he couldn't get a job driving here."

"When was the last time you saw him?"

"Two weeks ago. He stopped in on his way out of town. He had a load from Omaha and wanted some free room and loving. I wouldn't let him stay. I've been done with him for several months; I found out he was hitting on one of the girls I work with!"

"What made you write him? Did something happen before he left?"

"No...nothing. I just didn't want him around here anymore."

I identify who I am and where I am from. Then hand her a copy of the letter. "Is this the letter you sent him?"

That does it. She breaks down into spasms of sobbing and tears. "Oh God, am I going to go to jail because I didn't report him? I wanted him gone, away, never to come back."

Greg steps up and tells her because they're still married, she cannot testify against him anyway. She just needs to tell us what she knows.

"After I sent him away, I went to work as usual. Around ten that night a woman crawled through the emergency room doors, bleeding profusely. I immediately called for a nurse, then I went over to the poor woman and tried to comfort her. She was shaking uncontrollably. I attempted to keep her still, but she was babbling on about how this trucker smashed her head when she demanded her money after they'd had sex. The woman said she almost passed out but then started to scream. The driver, Bill was his name, told her to shut up and started hitting her again with something heavy. He kept driving and hitting her. She opened the passenger door, jumped out, and fell to the roadway. She saw the hospital sign, and stumbling and crawling, made it to the ER doors. As I held her, she passed out. She never regained consciousness. I never told the ER staff what the woman said."

We talk with Gloria awhile. "Bill has been a trucker for several years. I've been with him around two years. We met when he was a patient in the hospital. He had an accident nearby and was being treated in the Enid Hospital. One thing led to another and I took him in while he was recovering. We got married. He seemed like such a kind person back then. Boy, was I wrong and stupid I guess too. He was working for a company out of Tulsa and Enid made a good base for him. He was home at least once a week. That's a good deal for a long-haul trucker. Everything was fine with Bill and me until one of my co-workers asked if we were still married. Seems my loving husband had been asking my co-worker for a date while he was waiting for me to get off shift. That was it for me. I sent Bill packing. I only had the PO box number in California as a forwarding address." She knew nothing of the domestic disturbances he had been involved in locally. Boy's a player. She seems like a good person but a little naive in her choice of a husband.

After conferring with Greg's boss, we go to the truck stop to see what leads, if any, we can develop. The boss is going to have a detective contact the women who called in the domestic complaints on Bill.

At the truck stop we meet up with an Oklahoma highway patrolman Greg knows. The officer is familiar with the local truckers and the "truck stop queens."

The patrolman says, "Don't remember running into Weaton. I notice the names on the trailers, as well as the fancy painted rigs. Part of my job. The Brown Freight Company trailer from Stockton rings a bell with me. It was dirty, looked in questionable shape; I was thinking of stopping it for a safety inspection when I was dispatched to an accident." According to the officer, that was a couple of weeks ago.

Whoa, another coincidence. This is Weaton territory; I can almost smell him. He could still be around, but after narrowly getting shot, I doubt it. That was too close.

The highway patrolman talks with the "girls" in the coffee shop at the truck stop. This is where they hang out. He finds a couple who know of Bill. They say he is bad news. Gets too rough and will try to hold back on the money.

Greg and I talk with the truck stop employees. We find one of the station attendants who saw Weaton early this morning. He was fueling up and heading out to Florida. Checking the charge receipts, we find he is working for a trucking company from Utah. So Weaton has found another job. Now we have a name on the trailer for the APB.

Back at the office, we call the Utah Freight Line. They lease the trailers and don't have them marked. It will take some time to get the license number for us. Great, the bastard merrily drives away from us not knowing how close he was to handcuffs.

Chapter 13

There is not much more to do in Enid, Oklahoma. The detectives have spoken with the victims from Weaton's earlier escapades. They met him in various local bars, knew he was a truck driver, but not much else. One-night stand kind of things.

After a final night of merriment with the local cops, I go back home.

Now it is back to business as usual. My cases have been piling up. Apparently, everyone else is too busy to take even one of mine. That's how it goes. Heading to the chief's office to update him on the Enid trip, I'm nervous. I had made a lot of progress, but I also feel Weaton slipped through my fingers while I was in town.

The chief sits back in his chair, furrows his brow, and gets a stern look on his face as I report on the trip. "Damn, so close. Keep plugging, Bob; you will get him. Sounds like you did all the right things. The Enid people were good to you, it seems. That's how it should be."

I leave his office and start to breathe again. Where is the yelling and screaming I always heard he did? I know nobody wants to work the south county, so I can do no wrong. Probably not the case, but I'm going with it.

The district attorney issues a murder warrant for

Weaton. Apparently, I had enough evidence to get his attention. Enid, Oklahoma does not, but they are following it up thoroughly.

I go about my routine cases and keep checking on Weaton. The Utah freight company finally gets back to me with a license number on their trailer. By then it has been dropped off in Florida. Thanks, guys. Appreciate the effort to combat crime. They also inform me Weaton is no longer employed. He chose not to continue with them. Great, now he is virtually invisible again.

A few days later the Georgia finance company calls me. They have been advised Weaton sold his truck and they'll be receiving their money. He sold it to a dealer in Florida but took a hit financially because of the arrears payments. I get the Florida truck dealer's name and call.

The salesman tells me Weaton wanted to get rid of the truck and was going to become a company driver. No more owner-operator. This is a possibility, but I think it's more likely he's getting nervous.

Then I remember his driver's license is coming up for renewal. He needs to become visible for that to happen, even for a short period of time. This is a window for me. The national CDL-commercial drivers' license program is now coming online. I can find him when he applies for his now *required* nationwide license. I'm excited by the prospect, though something inside me says it isn't going to work.

Six months later, it has not worked. No sign of Weaton on any CDL or any state's driver's license listing. I even try Canada, to no avail. What is he doing? All he knows is truck driving. Something is not right with this picture.

I check in with Greg in Enid occasionally. He's been keeping tabs on Gloria. Perhaps a little more than professional follow-up, Greg? I only saw her the one time, but she was not at her best. With a good night's sleep and a shower...maybe not too bad. Anyway, neither she nor Greg have heard anything of Weaton. I update him on what I have found out. He says it doesn't make sense.

"Everybody has to drive, don't they?"

Then it hits me. Yes, they do, but what if...he is no longer Weaton?

I hang up with Greg and go immediately to our dispatch center. The dispatchers handle all our record checks. They have access to all kinds of national records, databases, etc. We are getting into the computer era now. Information is easier to obtain and quicker.

The dispatch center is located on a hill overlooking the town. This is where all our radio traffic comes from and goes to when we are in our cars. Smart officers make friends here. Can be beneficial sometimes. The dispatchers receive a lot of donuts and candy. Well deserved, might I add.

I go to the records section. This is where the data comes from. I talk with the supervisor I've dealt with for several years. She is a great dispatcher and helped me out many times. Now I am asking for information, not backup or directions to someplace not on the map. I want her to search the nationwide data bases for Weaton. But not just Weaton. I don't know what to tell her about any search parameters. That's the problem. I know he's out there somewhere in electronic land; I just don't know what to look for besides his basics: name, SSN, DOB, the usual. I do that constantly. I tell the supervisor what I have and what I am trying to find.

She looks at me. "Did my boss tell you to find some hopeless task for me, since he thinks I don't have enough work to do?" Then she laughs. "Leave me the information; I'll see what I can come up with in my spare time. Candy's not going to cover this one."

I promise her "anything" if she can help me out. I fill her in on the details of the cases. She starts to ask questions; I can see the mind spinning. She's hooked now. She calls me several times over the next couple of weeks. Nothing is coming up. Finally, she says, "Are you sure he's still a truck driver and still alive? I have tried every place and database I can think of. He does not exist anymore in any public record."

I know what he has done...he has changed identities. He does not exist publicly, but someone else does. He had to find someone of similar physical characteristics and take over the person's identification. Now we need to search for *recently deceased males of his basic description.* I tell the supervisor what I am thinking and ask her to check on recently issued CDLs. He would need to use the deceased's ID to get one.

"Oh, now this is really going to cost you; the price just went way up."

In the meantime, I keep working my assigned cases and try not to think of Weaton, but I cannot let it go. I could have passed him on the streets of Enid and not known. It truly bothers me. I keep checking with Greg. He has no new leads. I tell him my latest theory. He agrees it's plausible.

Even Charlie has no guidance for me. He says, "He

entered a monastery and has repented for his life of sin."

"Go back to your strawberries."

"What?"

"Never mind."

Months pass and William Weaton has disappeared off the public records of the world. The list of recently deceased fitting his general description is skimpy. It is not that they don't exist, it's just the records don't always show up. Agencies all over the country are changing over to newer computer systems and some of the data is not converted right away, if at all.

I check out each one as I get time. Most are traffic accidents, but some are an occasional act of violence thrown in for good measure. Jealous husband, jealous wife, or bar fights. Nothing fits my criteria.

One evening I'm watching cable TV. For some reason I have on a Chicago super station; it's part of my package. I rarely watch it. Tonight, it has a news broadcast and as I am about to switch channels, they show a man's photo. He is missing and his family is trying to locate him. The photo looks enough like Weaton to be his twin. I feel my body inadvertently twitch in reaction to the picture. He was a truck driver, and his family has not heard from him for months. This was not too unusual, they say. They were not close, but his mother's birthday came and went without hearing from him. The family called the authorities. *He always called his mother on her birthday, no matter what.*

I digest this and take notes. Could it be? William has found his twin and assumed his identity? But where is the real guy? Two truckers disappearing who look similar. Curious.

The next day I call the TV station and get the name and basic info from them. It was reported from a small town outside of Chicago. I call the PD.

The detective in charge says they have absolutely nothing to go on. The family does not know what company he was driving for or where he might have gone. Since he is an adult and has lived a nomadic lifestyle, the police aren't too aggressive about working this case. I get his identifying information and call the dispatch supervisor.

"Finally, something I can get my teeth into." She sounds excited.

David Allen Colton is two years younger than William Weaton, but the DMV photo and picture I received from the Illinois police look close enough for them to be brothers.

I place a call to the family and speak to David's sister. She seems to be the motivating force behind their concern. "My brother, David, has been the black sheep of the family. After his wild teenage years, he settled down as a long-haul truck driver. As far as we know, he has not been in any trouble. He just prefers to be a loner. He would show up every few months, then the time frames began to get further apart. But he never missed Mom's birthday. Never. Until this year." Her voice breaks into sobs, "He would always call her."

That was when she called the police. The family never knew what company he drove for. When he did show up it would always be in a different truck. She didn't think he owned his own truck but preferred to drive for a large company. The sister says he kept away from the family because he and his dad had some bad times when he was growing up, and they never patched things up. I ask a few more questions but get no leads. David grew up in a small town and never left until he began driving trucks. No military service, so he took to the excitement of seeing the country from behind the wheel of a truck. He absolutely loved it.

The records show David Allen Colton's current CDL was issued in Nebraska, two years ago. It's valid for six more years. If Weaton aka Colton behaves himself, no accidents, or tickets, I may never find him until the six-year renewal period. The trucking companies do not report new hires. At the renewal, a ten-year history must be provided. The next six years I can only periodically check to see if he surfaces somewhere. At the end of six years, then what—another "missing" driver of similar appearance?

Chapter 14

Driving back to the station from an investigation, I get an epiphany. I do not think I ever had one before; they don't hurt, just kind of jar you. Sort of a "hey dummy, what about…?" I may have had them before; I didn't know what they were called until I read about them somewhere. Now I have epiphanies. Excellent.

My great idea is to flood the truck stops and everywhere I can think of with David Allen Colton's photo. *Brilliant; what took me so long?* The long-haul drivers travel the country, and they are their own *social network.* I have learned they do not have much outside world contact. The other drivers via the CB radios in their trucks, the employees at truck stops, and the personnel at freight terminals are about it for them.

I get the approval from my boss to do the project. He even has helpful ideas for me. Okay, who is this guy? I worry about being stuck in the south county. It is not that I don't like the area; in fact, I'm quite comfortable. Know my way around and have a lot of contacts; it is working out for me. The problem is, how can I advance if I am only the "south county" boy? I feel I need to be in a more populated metropolitan area of the county.

Charlie looks at it differently. "You made the 'good' list with the cattle rustling caper and if you pull off this one, you're as good as gold for another promotion."

"You made a lot of great busts in your career and retired an investigator."

"By choice, son, by choice. I didn't want any of the politics that go with promotions. I just wanted to do my job, my way."

"Okay, Frank Sinatra...yes, you did."

"Thank you, smart-ass. When you get those flyers printed up, give me some. It'll give me an excuse to drink coffee at truck stops again. The wife is killing me with her 'honey-dos.'"

Project Colton is under way. I have the flyers printed with both photos. The real Colton and I add Weaton's picture and information. Since he now has a warrant out on him, he is fair game, and the more publicity the better. I do not say Weaton is responsible for Colton's disappearance, but it is implied. How's that for vague innuendo?

Between us, Charlie, bless his heart, and I cover the truck stops in the area. Some truck stops are chains and I get the manager to fax a flyer to the corporate office, which is more than willing to help. Talking to truckers while I am there, I find these guys and ladies are quite anxious to help. They see Colton/Weaton as a real danger to them. They will pass out flyers on their routes.

Now I wait. Oh yes, I have my regular cases to work. After all, if the flyers do not turn up something, I have six more years to wait.

Out of the blue I get a call from the Elko County Sheriff's Office in Nevada. I'm excited as I return it. Maybe it's a break. After all, Interstate Highway 80 runs through Elko between both coasts. Big truck route.

My excitement is blown when I find out they are interested in cattle rustling. They heard about my case and wanted to share facts on one of their outstanding cases. Will my fame never stop shining? Price of glory. *Okay, stop it. Listen to the man and see if you can help.*

The lead detective is George who has a case of cattle rustling like the one I handled. He has a witness who saw a cattle hauler with California plates in the area of the theft. I assure him my boys are still in prison, but they did have some acquaintances who would not be above doing such things. I tell George I did not keep the names of the acquaintances. An FBI agent was looking for them; I merely facilitated the interview.

"Oh, great, now I have to ask the FBI for help?" George grumbles.

"He's not too bad, in fact, a regular guy. I had drinks with him."

"What'd he put in your drink?"

"No, honest. A good guy, like a real cop. Trust me."

George and I talk a while longer. We're like-minded about lots of things. He's a matter-of-fact cop with a "let's catch the bad guys" attitude like mine.

"Give me his number, I'll call him." He resigns himself to the inevitable.

Later FBI Andy calls me. He was able to give the Elko detective information on his persons of interest. Andy has not been able to prove these guys were involved in his theft from government property. He believes they're "good for it," though. Andy suggests lunch the next day. I am beginning to like him despite his job. But I'm going to watch my drink.

At lunch I fill him in on the Weaton case. "Give me a few of the flyers. I'll put them out to my agency. Why didn't you call me about this? I can help. After all, Weaton worked for a company doing interstate commerce; that's my kind of stuff."

They never quit, do they? The FBI wants to get in on everything. This is mine, damn it. *Okay, settle down.* He did not say he wants to take over the case; maybe he can help. But it's still *my case.*

True to his word, Andy gets the flyers national coverage. I'm not sure what will turn up, Weaton or another dead trucker. This seems the only way to go, make it public. Remember...*Everyone sees something. You just have to find them.*

Sure enough, I start getting phone calls about the flyers. Most are, "I remember meeting him," or "I seen a trucker last year looked jess like 'im." These do not help me, but the momentum has begun. I need current sightings or maybe even a body. I'm convinced the real Colton is in a bottomless mineshaft somewhere. *Probably not under first base at Yankee Stadium, I believe Jimmy Hoffa slid in there first.*

My boss is pleased with how I am handling the case; he loves the publicity and, of course, so does the sheriff. More important to me, Charlie is alive again. He is calling and offering suggestions and wanting updates. I get invited over for dinner occasionally. His wife takes me aside and says the case has pulled him out of the doldrums after he first retired. She thanks me for keeping him in the loop. I remind her Charlie's the reason I am where I am professionally. I will always be grateful to him.

Weeks go by. There are plenty of tips but no real

facts to follow up. I keep working my day job. I run the usual gauntlet of cases, court appearances, and all the normal detective stuff. But I am obsessed with Weaton/Colton.

One day good old Sarah tells me I have been selected to speak at a local high school vocation day.

I ask, "Who chose me and why?"

"I did, sweetie, because the chief told me to get some detectives who were a good example of today's law enforcement to represent the agency, as an inspiration for today's youth. I picked one detective for each high school in the county."

"Sarah, you are so full of it. There are X number of high schools and X number of detectives. Don't BS me; you just went down the list."

"Well, yes, but I gave you the one in a nicer area. I thought you would look good to them. At least I didn't send you to the South County schools."

"Thank you, Sarah."

Chapter 15

My day to shine comes, and I go to the high school. I am speaking at eleven a.m. to a bunch of high school seniors who can't wait to get to lunch. I can do this. In and out; they won't be paying attention anyway.

I bring my flyers along as an example of how small cases can quickly develop into much larger ones. The group I speak to is attentive and some even ask intelligent questions. I easily finish before lunch and am pleased with myself. As everyone is leaving the room a student comes up to me and asks if she can talk to me. Sure, why not, that's why I'm here.

Pointing at my flyer she says, "I think I've seen him." She is pointing at Weaton's photo.

"You sure?"

"Well, I'm fairly sure. His face is a little distorted on the right side, but it sure looks like him in the eyes and nose. The hair line is the same."

I'm impressed; even if she is wrong, what an eye for detail. I sit her down and begin to ask her how and where she saw him.

"My sister may be dating him. She lives in Reno and I went to see her with my parents a few weeks ago. He's a truck driver. My sister works in a casino, near a truck stop. That's how they met." She says the right side of his face doesn't look the same as the left, like he had an accident or something. I ask her about the picture of Colton, and she says it's not the same person—similar, but not the same.

"So you met him?"

"Oh yeah, he's...I think...living with my sister or was then."

"What was his name?"

"Al."

Holy crap. If Weaton got his face banged up, maybe while murdering David Alan Colton, this could be him. Just when I had almost lost faith in today's youth this kid comes along. I have got to be very careful how I proceed from here. If "Al" is Weaton, we do not want the sister tipped off yet. But she could be in danger. I tell the girl my fears. We must proceed carefully, to protect her sister, in case it is Weaton.

"Won't be the first loser she's hooked up with."

I ask her how her parents would take this news and the police involvement.

"My parents worry; they're afraid she's going down the wrong path. She is and has been for the last few years. Drinking, smoking, and gambling. I don't think drugs, yet."

"You close to her, talk much?"

"Yeah, at least twice a month. My parents can't talk to her without yelling at her. You're worried if my parents know they will call her and chase him off, so you can't catch him, huh? But you're also worried she'll be in danger if he knows, right?"

"Smart girl; you want to be a police officer when you finish college?"

"Actually, I want to be an FBI special agent."

"That hurts."

"Nothing personal, but last week we had this FBI

agent, Andy, speak to us. He told us all about what they do and how they travel the world. That's what I want to do."

Damn it. Next time *he* buys dinner and I am going to put something in *his* drink.

This is a touchy situation. I have a minor who comes to me of her own volition with information. If her parents know about this and say anything to her sister, she will likely be in danger. Weaton/Colton could possibly kill her to wipe out any leads to him. The girl offers to give me her sister's address, phone number, and place of employment. She understands the danger to her sister and is afraid of her parents' reaction.

"Do they have to know? I love my stupid sister and don't want anything to happen to her. Can't you go check it out and get him, if it's him, and they won't even have to know I was involved?"

"Under the circumstances I think that would be the best way to handle it," I reply. I was going to say she needs to take a breath, but she is not in the mood for a joke.

I give her my number. The young lady is going to call with her sister's information. I promise not to tell her parents. We are not supposed to question a minor without their parents' consent, but in this case, she came to me.

I go to the chief. He agrees with me. The parents need to stay out of this one. The student will only be referenced as an anonymous informant in the final report. He tells me to let him know when I have the sister's information. He'll call Reno PD to arrange to have them work with me. Boy, this detective stuff does have its moments. A trip to Reno.

The next day the student calls as promised. She gives me all the information I need to proceed.

I tell the chief, who gets on the phone to Reno and talks to someone he has dealt with in the past. After a few minutes of old-boy-BS, he gets down to business. Within five minutes I am on the phone with the detective who will be working with me. I'll be driving up there tomorrow. He tells me he will arrange for a hotel for me at a professional rate. The chief say it will probably be free. The hotels want to stay on good terms with the police, so law enforcement personnel get special consideration. He has obviously been there before.

I leave in the afternoon. It's only a four or five hour drive. Pleasant this time of year, no snow. I arrive and check in at the hotel, a good place downtown. I call the detective, Mike Harper. He says to wait in the casino lounge, he will be there in twenty minutes. Better than a coffee shop. Mike shows up and I can spot a fellow police officer a mile away. Clean-cut guy, an air of confidence, and a slight bulge on his side, under the untucked shirt. Declares he is off work and suggests we order up a drink. So we do. I had given him a briefing on the phone, and he has already done some checking around. He knows the personnel officer at the casino and confirmed the sister is still employed there. She's a waitress on day shift—six a.m. to two p.m.—in the coffee shop. He drove by her home, a rental in an older part of town. No vehicle in front and no one in sight. Commercial trucks are not allowed to park on the city streets, so that was no help. We need dinner. He suggests a nice place a few minutes away. It is a *very nice* place. As we walk in, a large man in a dark suit, the maître d', greets Mike warmly. He is obviously a regular here, and also currently single. Like too many of us in law enforcement.

We have a great dinner, wine, and all. Genuinely great. When the bill comes Mike insists on paying. He will not hear my protests. "You get lunch tomorrow," he says. After this dinner I am not sure where lunch will be, but I am glad my plastic is in good standing.

After we finish, Mike suggests we drive by the sister's place to check. Okay, we've been drinking and trying to work may not be a good idea.

"Just a drive-by," he says. "It's summer, maybe the windows will be open, and we can see who's inside." He means Weaton, of course. And if he is, then what?

No ones in sight at the house, much to my relief. Mike lets me off at my hotel. He will pick me up at eight in the morning.

Chapter 16

After Mike picks me up, we head to where the sister works. We cruise the truck stop parking lot looking for anyone who is similar in appearance to our suspect. Nothing. We go inside the truck stop's main building. There's a drivers' lounge, showers, pay phones and a coffee shop. This is not where the sister works. She's nearby in the main casino's coffee shop. On a bulletin board with all sorts of trucker info is my flyer. Someone has written on it: "Let's find this bastard."

I'm impressed.

No one in here looks anything like our guy so we head over to the casino. From the little sister's description, it's easy to spot her sister. She's working the counter and some booths. We sit in her section and when she comes over, we order coffee. The place is quiet. When she brings our coffee, I tell her we are police officers, and ask if she'd mind looking at a couple of photos.

"Sure."

She's calm and doesn't seem at all nervous talking to cops. After all, who hangs out here more than cops and truckers?

I pull out separate photos of Weaton and Colton, not my flyer. I show her Weaton first.

"Oh my god!" She almost drops the coffee pot.

"He looks just like Alan, except his cheekbone; it sticks out more."

I tell her I think the picture was taken before his accident. She sits down in the booth and holds the photo.

"What'd he do?" Tears begin to fill her eyes.

I tell her we're not sure of anything yet and show her Colton's photo.

"He looks a little like Alan, but who is he? Is he the one you're looking for?"

"We're looking for both. When was the last time you saw Alan?" I closely watch for her reaction.

"Just this morning. I dropped him off at the truck stop; he was leaving for St. Louis. He came in night before last and stayed with me until this morning."

"Who does he drive for? Can you describe his truck?" I'm getting excited. He's close.

"I don't know, I've never seen his truck. He always meets me here or at the truck stop building."

"You have never seen his truck. Come on, how long have you known him?"

"I met him about six months ago. He came in here to eat. A lot of the drivers like to eat in the casino and gamble. We hit it off and I stayed after my shift. One thing led to another and I took him home. He would stay a day or so and then go on his run to wherever. When he was coming through Reno, he would call me and I would meet him, if I wasn't working."

"Does he have a regular route?"

"No, he could be going to anywhere from anywhere. Sometimes he comes by every week or two and sometimes not for a month or more; that's how it is with long-haul truckers, you know."

"Where did he come from this time?"

"He said he picked up his load in San Jose. It's where my family lives. I told him he should have called them while he was there. He met them two weeks ago when they came here to visit. Probably just as well, my folks, especially my father, didn't take to him too well."

She must wait on some customers and asks us to please stay. *Believe me, my dear, we are going nowhere!*

San Jose...couple of flipping days ago. Son of a bitch. I was there, I live there, the monster was right there in my city.

We watch as she goes back to work. She does not leave the room to use a pay phone, so she's not trying to warn him. If he's on the road again, she can't.

"What do you think?" Mike asks.

"I pretty much believe her, but wouldn't she ever wonder why she never saw his truck?"

When she comes back, we again go over the unseen truck issue. She says she has dated several truckers and yes, most of them like to be dropped off at their rig. But he always said he left his logbooks and load papers in a locker at the truck stop for safety. She said the drivers use the lockers for their valuables rather than leaving them in the truck. Then she gets a serious look on her face.

"He did something, didn't he? When he got here two days ago and sat down at the counter, I didn't recognize him at first. He'd colored his hair black and was growing a beard. He was wearing a grubby sweatshirt with the hood up. He never dressed that way before. I asked him why and he said he was tired being the all-American boy with his blond hair and clean-cut look."

"You bought that?" I say.

"Hey, these guys are alone a lot and some of them get weirder as time goes by. I thought maybe it was his time. I also thought it might be time not to see him anymore. He'd always want to go out and party but this time he stayed at my place, watched TV, and drank."

"Was he mean or abusive to you?" Mike asks.

"No, never. He was always very nice and gentle. But there was one time when we were out drinking, he damn near killed some guy. I got him out of there before the police came."

"What happened? "Mike says.

"A man came up to him and said he looked like someone; I didn't really hear it. I was getting drunk myself. Alan unloaded on him. I grabbed him and pulled him outside and got him into my car. He never told me exactly what the guy said or why he was so crazy mad."

"When was this?" I ask.

"Two weeks ago. After my parents left, we went out to the casino for dinner and you know, some drinking."

Okay, now we are getting somewhere. He gets recognized by someone while he is out in public with her and then tries to disguise himself. He would have seen the flyers in the truck stops, too. He knows we're on to him.

I show her the flyer. She studies it carefully. Then she starts to cry. "It's him, isn't it? Oh God, Oh God, it's him, it's him. I didn't know, I didn't know."

The manager comes toward us. Mike tells him who we are. He explains we had to bring some bad news to his waitress and she has done nothing wrong. He seems cool with this. He says she can take the rest of the day off.

After she calms down somewhat, we ask her to remember anything that might give us a hint to any connections he might have to other places. She says he was from Georgia with no family left. His folks died when he was younger and had no other family he knew of or cared about.

We get her back to her house and she seems to be taking it in stride now. "Live and learn, I guess. I've gotta do better than this, truckers, drinking, gambling. Maybe I should take my parents up on their offer to come home and find a job there. Waitresses can always get work. I gotta stay away from truck stops." She wipes away a few tears with the back of her hand.

Mike gives her his phone number and says he'll check on her daily until she does move. She says this has been a wakeup call and thanks us. I hope she means it.

Now Mike and I huddle. We don't know exactly what we are looking for. He will not be out of the state by now if he left when she said he did. I get one of those bright ideas of mine that hurts. *Dumb fool, he must fuel up sometime.* You know how this works; you have done it before in Enid. Talk to the attendants at the fuel station at the truck stop.

Before we leave the sister, I have her draw what his hair and beard look like now on one of my flyers. On another one, I add the hooded sweatshirt and facial hair.

We go to the attendants and cashiers who are on duty this morning. No one saw him today. One of them remembers someone who fueled up a couple of days ago dressed in a hooded sweatshirt and thought it was odd since it is summer and hot. He couldn't remember what truck line it was, just how odd the guy looked. We call the sister and ask if she can remember exactly when he arrived. She thinks about it and says it was after one p.m.; she told him she would be getting off shift in about an hour. He told her he'd gotten in a couple of hours before and would wait for her. We go back to the fuel cashier to try and pin down the time frame against the charge slips. It was busy, no less than eighteen fill-ups during that time period. No way to determine which areas the truckers were coming from.

A dead end. Eighteen trucks fueled up two days ago and one of them is now on I-80 headed toward Utah, along with thirty to fifty others. After talking with a Nevada highway patrol trooper, we see no way of finding our needle in the haystack. The trooper has seen the flyer and is on the lookout for my guy, as are the other troopers. It is posted in each of their offices. Quite a campaign I've got going.

Chapter 17

Reno was a dead end. He is on the road to somewhere. Maybe St. Louis or somewhere else. He may not have told the sister the truth. He's getting cagey now. The pressure is building on him.

What's he going to do now? How long can he keep this up? His company will watch his CDL renewal date and will not worry much about him if he does his job, doesn't have an accident, or get too many tickets. He will keep altering his appearance. My flyers are haunting him.

I run weekly records check for any tickets or other public records for either Weaton or Colton.

About a week after I return from Reno, the little sister calls me and thanks me for "saving her dumb sister." Apparently, the woman called the parents and asked to come home.

I tell the girl she saved her sister by coming forward. *Good kid, even if she may turn out to be a member of the evil FBI.*

The months go by, tips come in, but none are fruitful. I manage to get the National Trucking Association to send the flyer with its updated images to their members. This includes the major trucking companies throughout the country. Just maybe someone at the companies will check their employees' names against the flyer. More pressure.

I'm doing well at my job. Time flies by. The agency seems pleased with me, my evaluations are all good, even an occasional "above standard." I have been made a Detective II, which is a little better pay. I'm happy. I've even been dating. Nothing serious so far, but at least I have other things to do besides drink with the guys. The wives of the married ones are also happy, though I don't think for the same reasons as me.

One day I get a phone call from George with the Elko County Sheriff's Office in Nevada.

"George, how're you doing?" I greet him. "Sorry, but I don't have any more cattle rustling cases at the moment."

"You know we handle more than cattle rustling up here. We can even do our job without the FBI, but I must admit Andy was a big help on my case."

"Glad to hear it. I told you he was like a real cop."

"Yeah, he is. Listen the reason I called is more about you."

"Look, George, I was in Reno a few months ago, but I never got close to Elko. I didn't do it; nobody saw me do it. I'm innocent. Do I need an attorney?"

When he stops laughing, he gets serious. "You ever think of coming to work in a real sheriff's office and getting out of the land of fruits and nuts?"

"I take it you're serious; you wouldn't waste the county's money on a long-distance joke, right?"

"Right, here's the deal. I have been made undersheriff. The bigger agencies are stealing our trained deputies as fast as they make probation, and we are hurting for experience. While I was the lieutenant in charge of investigations, I was also the lead detective, and sometimes the only detective. You would take the open lieutenant's position. Right now, I have two detectives with less time on the force than I have hair on my head. One of them will probably have to go back to patrol; he's not cut out for investigation."

"Why me? I realize Elko is a rural area, but you must have met someone else other than me, or don't you get out much?"

"Your humor is one of the reasons. When we talked before, I was impressed with your attitude and common-sense way of thinking about police work. We were able to work together and enjoy it. That's important, especially these days. Yes, smart-ass, I do get out a little and know others, but I'm recruiting you. Also, I am impressed with how you're handling your trucker murder suspect. Come up for a few days and I'll show you around. Then make your decision."

"How do you know about the trucker?"

"Every law enforcement officer along I-80 knows about it. We are all looking for him in every truck we see. I talked with Harper in Reno; he filled me in on your visit. Damn, you were close."

"You know Mike?"

"Yes, all of us out here are in contact with each other. The bad guys move along the highway you know. So when are you coming up?"

I have plenty of unused vacation time, so I will take a week off and go to Elko. Can't be hard to find. Go to Reno, head east on I-80, and eventually you find it. There must be road signs; it is at least that big, isn't it?

Obviously, I'm not being too serious about this. *Lieutenant,* I like the sound of that. But Elko County seems like our south county, only ten times bigger. I don't know if I'm ready for that. But "lieutenant;" might as well see what is there. Nothing ventured, nothing gained.

It's a pleasant drive from San Jose to Reno and a looong drive to Elko from Reno. A hot, long drive and not much scenery change. Sage brush and desert, that is it. I'm already wondering about this.

Elko spreads out in front of me as I hit the city limit sign. Well, more like kind of off to the right but there are a lot of homes, buildings, etc. The town's bigger than I thought. I see substantial mountains in the distance. They must be the famous Ruby Mountains.

I call George as I pull into the parking lot of the hotel he arranged for me. Oh yes, we are now into the era of cell phones for the common people. The county gave me one for work and I even purchased one. Nice, but my off-duty time is no longer my own. I can be called anytime. I guess that's progress. It used to be a pager, which you could always say, "I must have been out of range, etc." Now, not so simple.

George says his wife would like me to come to dinner. Great, he has the poor woman involved in this conspiracy.

I go at the appointed hour. Nice place a little way from town and more toward the hills. George has done well. He meets me at the door. If those detectives have less time on the force than he has hair, they must be children. He's almost bald. George is in his fifties, I guess. Good shape for his age; actually, exceptionally good shape. I wouldn't want to have to mess with him. His wife is gracious and offers me a beer. George already has one. Okay, so far. Dinner's great; home cooking is always a pleasure for me. They ask me about myself. George more guy stuff and her more personal things...any girlfriend or children? The kind of things women always want to know. I can see she's sizing me up for blind dates. Women think being alone is unacceptable and they have a moral duty to help.

George talks up the department, locale, clean air, good hunting and fishing, etc. I break it to him that I am more into sports cars and auto racing than the other stuff. Doesn't break his stride at all. "That's a nice Porsche you have; what year is it?"

"1976, that's my baby," I say proudly.

"Actually, it looks brand new. They must be good in the snow, being from Germany and all."

Yes, George, I know Elko has snow, another item on the negative side of my list. Other than the lieutenant position and George's wife's cooking, I don't have many positives.

We talk for some time. George and I hit it off well. We decide to meet in the morning; George will show me the sheriff's office and the Elko area.

I wind up staying four days. It is a nice area, I must admit. The nearby Ruby Mountains are beautiful. Elko, not so much, but George sees I meet the nicest people and the important ones. I meet the sheriff, who almost fawns over me. *You guys are desperate, aren't you?* I've met several deputies, sergeants, and a captain. All look good to me, so what's the problem? The problem, George says, for the most part they work their shift and then go home, or go hunting, fishing or whatever. Detectives are on call a lot. These guys, and one genuinely nice lady I met, just want to do their job and be able to enjoy their time off duty.

The lady, who has been on the department for

fourteen years, started out a matron in the jail and became the first female deputy. She takes me aside one day and tells me George and the sheriff are good to work for. She says, "You do your job, and they'll back you up. They have for me and everyone else who works hard. They won't throw you to the political wolves."

I think her life has been rough; first female deputy in a basically redneck cow county. She seems so down-to-earth and, well, pleasant.

I mention this to George later; he laughs. "She's one tough cookie. The local boys know better than to hassle her. I'd take her with me to any call."

****

On my last day George brings me into the sheriff's office again. After the usual pleasantries, the sheriff says, "Now here's the deal." He looks directly at me. "As George has pointed out to you, I'm sure, we are understaffed and under-experienced, if there is such a word, and while we have some very good deputies, we have no one suited to head our investigation unit. The experienced deputies and sergeants like it where they are. The new ones are just too new. George has done some checking on you and likes what he sees. With personnel rules as they are, the only way to hire someone is by the usual exam, etc. However, I can bring in an outsider for a department head position. The Board of Supervisors has already approved this. They are painfully aware of our staffing problems. I am formally offering you the position of lieutenant to head up the investigation unit. While we may be short on staff, the county has good operating capital, and we would move you at our expense."

I sit there, trying to mull this all over in my mind. I

did not expect to be offered anything formally yet. I figured they were looking at me, as I was looking at them.

Before I can say anything, the sheriff raises his hand toward me. "Go on home; take a few days to consider all the pros and cons. I know this is a cultural change for you. George is confident you will do well here. So am I."

****

The next morning, my Porsche and I take off for San Jose. I barely remember the drive to Reno; my head is still swimming. I give Mike Harper a call when I hit Reno. We have lunch.

"You going to take it?"

"I don't know. I have been thinking about it so much I have a headache. I'm just going to go back to work and let it all settle in."

"Personally, for what it's worth, I think you should take it. George probed me about the job, and I told him I was a city boy and Elko was way too far out for me. I suggested you, being a county guy and all, and he said you were next on his list. I take it you've worked together in the past. He likes you even after spending a week with you."

"Four days."

"Whatever; he likes you."

Chapter18

I make it back home. I have a message on my phone. I don't think I feel like partying tonight, guys, but wait, maybe it is a female offering companionship. So I hit the play button.

"Are you going to take it?"

Charlie. Damn, does he know everything? I never told him about going to Elko. I call him back; maybe I will at least get dinner out of this.

His wife answers. "Oh Bob, Charlie's at the store, but he'll be right back. Would you like to come over for dinner tonight?"

"Sure, I always enjoy your cooking, even if I have to put up with Charlie."

"I put up with the dear all the time. How about seven?"

Okay, now she's in on this. I wonder which way old Charlie is going on it. Only one way to find out. I show up at seven with a bottle of her favorite wine.

Charlie wastes no time getting to the point. "Are you going to become a lieutenant in Elko?"

"How do you know about this?" I ask, indignant.

"George called me; we go back years. Good man. What are you going to do?"

"I don't know yet, I'm still weighing it." I know I do not need to ask for his input. I will get his opinion, forthwith.

And here it comes. "You'd be a fool not to jump on it. It'll open a host of doors for your future in other places. You're still young enough to go anywhere you want."

"But you had no use for promotions."

"That's me. You're different. You are a good cop, and you can navigate through the brass and politics, but still get the job done. Take it, son."

****

Okay, now I am back to work and still haven't decided. I try to put it out of my mind for a few days to let the dust settle. Fortunately, fate steps in to take my mind off this issue.

I'm on the road starting to work the cases that piled up while I was gone (*thanks again everyone; wait until you go on vacation*). I receive a radio call, robbery in progress, at a mom-and-pop store in my area. Mack and Marie Romero own it. A patrol car is only a few minutes away and I tell him my ETA is five minutes. I ask patrol to ease up to the side of the building out of sight, then cover the front and I will hit the rear. I know this location from my patrol days. A lumberyard is next door; I can sneak through their lot and go to the back of the store without being seen. Unfortunately, just as the deputy pulls to the side of the store, the suspect runs out the front door, sees the patrol car, and runs back inside. The deputy radios me with this information. I am easing up to the back door when it flies open and the suspect charges out, pushing Marie ahead of him. She falls to the ground. He has a gun. From inside the store, the deputy yells at him to halt. The suspect turns toward the open door and raises his gun.

"Police! Drop it or I'll blow your head off!" I yell.

He starts to turn toward me.

"Drop it now!"

Wisely, he drops it. The deputy comes out and handcuffs the suspect. Mrs. Romero is unharmed but scared. Her husband is at a doctor's appointment. I get her inside and call Mack at his doctor's office. I tell him what happened and reassure him Marie's fine. I take the report and pretty much open and close a case in one day: heck, one hour. Not bad. Good stats for me. The chief of detectives will be happy, too. Oh shit, I could be a lieutenant of detectives. *Stop it—you are not to be thinking about that for a few days.*

My old sergeant comes by, along with a small posse of responding deputies, highway patrol, etc. The deputy and I get all sorts of high-fives and pats on the back. The sergeant says I'm going to be the next sergeant after this, the rustling arrests, and the trucker case.

"You're doing great, son. Keep it up and you'll go far."

I do not think he's thinking as far as Elko and I'm not either now. I am modestly...well sort of...basking in my own glory. I know these are fleeting moments, but I am enjoying it. I know tomorrow the usual office politics could appear. But for now, this is nice.

I'm not considering Elko too seriously. Things are looking good here. We don't have snow, except in the mountains, and icy roads are not a concern. A little rain and fog, that's about it for weather problems. Yeah...well...the infrequent earthquake.

Little did I knew how quickly it would all go up in a puff of smoke.

In the afternoon, the chief of investigations calls a

meeting. This is not unusual. Occasionally he or the administration has some pearl of wisdom to pass on to the troops.

We all gather in our usual rowdy manner in the conference room. The chief and the personnel director come in and ruin our day. The chief looks at all of us. "Gentlemen, after twenty-five years on the department, I'm retiring."

You could have heard the proverbial pin drop. The sucking of wind in the room almost collapsed the walls. We're stunned, to say the least. Sure, he has been here a long time, but there was no hint he was even thinking of quitting. His announcement is met with a resounding, "Why?" Rude and selfish on our part perhaps, but despite his gruffness, he looked after his people.

With tears coming to his eyes, the chief reveals, "My wife has been diagnosed with cancer. I want to spend whatever time there is with her. She has supported me in this crazy business for years; now it's my turn."

There is not a dry eye in the room.

He gathers himself up, somberly looks at us again, and announces, "Chief Jim Broderick from civil division will be taking my place." He looks down and quietly says what sounds like, "May God have mercy on your souls," then quickly leaves the room.

The personnel director tells us we will be meeting with our new boss tomorrow at 0900 sharp. Then he beats a hasty retreat. He can sense what's coming.

For a minute no one says anything. We all absorb the news.

Then the room erupts. "Jim Broderick. The devil himself!" Chief Broderick is the most hated division chief in the sheriff's office. He used to be patrol commander. Rumor has it he was put into the civil division because of threats of assassination from his patrol deputies. An exaggeration, but he apparently had that effect on his officers. He caused a mass exodus of officers to other agencies. My own hiring into the department position was made available because of an experienced deputy leaving in disgust. That's disturbing. My present, quite wonderful lot in life is due to this terrible administrator.

Everyone talks at once. "Is San Jose hiring? How about Santa Clara city, Fremont, anybody?"

I'm rethinking Elko. Big time. A little snow, ice, not so bad after all, maybe.

When I get home, I do some research on Elko County. Seventeen thousand square miles compared to 1,300 for Santa Clara County. Wow, I knew it was bigger, but I did not realize how much bigger. I could spend the rest of my career trying to see all of it.

Okay, calm down. You're doing quite well here now. You have worked for difficult bosses before. Give him a try at least. Tomorrow is your first meeting with him. See how it goes.

****~

We all gather in the conference room; the mood is not optimistic. Many of the veterans worked under him in Patrol. I try not to listen to them. It must be my own decision.

Chief Broderick walks into the room exactly at 0900. He sits at a table at the front of the room and begins, "Good morning," in a voice much too loud for the size of the room. The guys in the civil division must be cheering now.

He starts right out by informing us the *old way* is gone. We will do things *his way* from now on. So much for easing into the job.

"First, your assignments will be changed. I think it's time to shake this stagnant unit up and start getting it running like a proper investigation department."

He then pulls out a paper and begins to reassign each of us. When he gets to me, he stops and stares right at me. "Carson, you'll be handling the North County cases. No more lollygagging around the unpopulated south. The area does not justify a full-time detective. Those cases will now be handled by the central unit. You're going to have to learn to pull your weight with a full load of cases. You can also stop chasing the mysterious truck driver who killed the whore. Not a priority. She asked for it. Otherwise, she wouldn't have been out there. Understood?"

"Understood." I am seething inside. *Why does he refer to my victim as a whore?* She was someone's daughter, caught up in a bad situation. This guy *is* the unfeeling jerk he has been made out to be. Maybe the assassination threats weren't just rumors.

We all finish the day, cleaning up our old cases as ordered. We met up at a coffee shop and basically cry in our beer, except it's coffee. Everyone wants out for sure now. No more "give him a chance." He showed his hand, and no one likes it. The desperation to find another home is rampant. I keep my mouth shut.

When I get home my phone rings; it's Charlie. "So, you going to go to Elko now?"

"It's beginning to look a lot more inviting. Did you know about the chief retiring?"

"Sarah called me. She was the only one in the unit

who was told."

Of course, another of Charlie's sources.

"Better give George a call; he can't wait forever. They need help up there, might as well be your help."

"Okay, tomorrow."

"Now."

"Now? It's after five."

"Now."

"Yes, sir."

I call Undersheriff George and guess what? He is in the office.

I tell him I will take the position. He seems relieved and then right away goes into the logistics. How soon can I start? He wants my address so he can have a mover notified. He'll be sending me insurance papers and whatever else the moving company needs. Fill them out and send them right back.

I hang up and do not feel relieved or whatever I'm supposed to feel. This is not how I want to move on. I feel like it is beyond my control. Maybe it is, maybe I am meant to go to Nevada.

Chapter 19

Now I'm forced to get my butt in gear and do things, like give my notice, pack, decide what goes, what gets donated, etc. George gave me whatever time I needed but would prefer two or three weeks. Two weeks' notice is all I'm required to give, so that will be it. It hasn't started to snow up north yet, I'm pleased. I need a place to live and coincidently, George knows of a nice little house for rent. He faxes me photos. Looks good and the rent is less than I'm paying for my apartment now. Has a two-car garage. That is the selling point. Porsche won't have to sit outside in the cold. Speaking of the weather, I guess I better buy snow chains. Crap.

I go in the office the next day and walk up to Sarah. Resignation in hand.

"I need to see the chief."

"Bob, come in," yells out the "old chief" from inside his office.

"Uh, Chief, I didn't know if you were still here or not."

"Yeah, I'm going to finish out the week. What do you have there? Your resignation so you can go to Elko?" He smiles and reaches for the paper.

"Am I the last to know?" I ask.

"Pretty much, yes. George called me a while ago. We all know each other, you realize."

"Apparently."

"Smart move, Bob. You will do a good job for them and they will look after you. It's a good thing. Especially now." He looks at me and winks.

"Thank you, Chief. I've enjoyed serving with you."

"See you at my party; it'll be a blowout!"

"Wouldn't miss it for the world, sir."

I ask him about his wife; he says she doing as good as can be expected. It'll be a rough road, he says, chemo and maybe radiation.

"She's a fighter; together we'll make it."

I go back to my desk. One week with the old chief and one with the new. I can make it. I'll try to leave my files in good order for the central unit who will have to take them over. Hope they don't lollygag around in the south county too much.

The other detectives are now so jealous of me, they can't stand it. "Who do you know in Elko?" Then the inevitable, "Need some help? Don't forget your old buddies." It goes on the whole two weeks. The poor guys are all scratching around trying to find some place to land. No one wants to stay. No one. We had a good unit.

The two weeks pass, and I am partied out by the time it's over. Dinner with the married guys and their wives. The wives are glad to see me leave. A couple nights out with the single ones. Of course, dinner with Charlie and his wife. I will miss Charlie, but I will deeply miss her cooking.

I am required to have an exit interview on my last day, but Broderick is too busy. The personnel director handles it.

"Good luck and thank you for your service for the

county." He then gets a sad look on his face. "You're only the first, I'm sure." He knows.

Then it is time.

The movers show up as scheduled. Not much in a bachelor pad. I put a few things in the Beast, my Porsche, and we head out. A quick stop for lunch in Reno with Harper and on to my future.

While driving across Nevada on I-80 for hours and hours, I keep thinking about "my case." It is *my case*, damn it. No one will work it, especially with Broderick's death knell. I cannot pass a truck without peering at the driver. Charlie says to keep checking now and again. He has done the same in the past on cases he could not let go. Sometimes it works out, sometimes it does not.

I call Undersheriff George as I'm getting close to Elko; he tells me to come to his house and we will go from there. I passed the moving van hours ago, so no sweat there.

It's dinner time and George's wife has prepared a delicious feast. I might freeze in Elko, but at least I won't starve. After dinner, the movers call and say they're close, so we go over to my house. It is a beautiful place. I'm pleased. Looks even better than the photos. Thanks, George, you did good.

After the movers leave, George goes home, and I spend my first night in my new home. George has seen to it the utilities are on and the cable TV is ready. He even stocked my fridge. Well, his wife did, he admits. Whoever; there's beer. I hook up my TV and grab a beer. I'm set for the first night, beer and TV.

George told me to take a few days to get adjusted and when I am ready, come on down to the office. This is all well and good, but now I am worried the other shoe will drop. Why are they so nice to me? What secret is here? What are they hiding? Once I start to work, will I never see the light of day again?

By three in the afternoon the next day, I'm bored. I have put my clothes away, gone to the store for more groceries, and even washed the Beast.

I show up at the sheriff's office unannounced. I want to see what is actually going on. I walk in the front door and the sheriff himself is walking down the hall.

"Bob, so glad you decided to join us." He throws out his hand and gives me a hearty shake. "You bored with this berg yet?"

I tell him I am, and he leads me to George's office.

"I didn't think it would take you too long; this is a small town. Ready to start?"

We go to personnel and I sign papers and then back to the sheriff's office to be sworn in and get my badge, ID, photos taken, all the usual stuff. Then I am shown to *my office*. Now this is freaky. My own office. We do not have enough staff, but apparently, we have plenty of room. I also have a vehicle assigned to me, not a new one, a late model 4wd SUV. Of course, it snows here. After being introduced to anyone I didn't meet the first trip, I'm handed the outstanding cases. My cases now.

Then a large man enters the room. George says, "Joseph, meet Bob, your new lieutenant."

Joseph is the "last detective standing" in the department. He has all of three years with the Elko force and two years with the tribal police department on a nearby reservation. Joseph's a Native American, shiny black ponytail and all. He shakes my hand with gusto.

"Man, am I glad to see you. I am way over my head here. I was ready to go back to Patrol, but George said to hang on, help was coming."

George leaves us to get acquainted.

"I thought there were two detectives?"

"Yeah, there were, but Harry went back to Patrol. He wasn't cut out for investigations. He likes his action, bar fights, tickets, all that stuff. I want to do this, but I feel like a duck out of water. George is the only reason I'm still here. He has taught me a lot, but he got promoted to undersheriff, and then it was just me. But now it's you and me." He smiles a big toothy smile at me.

"Well, Joseph, I bet we can get things done and close some cases together. What do you say?"

"Let's do it.'"

Chapter 20

Since I now have a county vehicle, I ask Joseph to drive it to my house and I will drive my Beast. When we go out to the parking lot Joseph sees my Porsche.

"I'll drive that one."

"Nice try, maybe later."

"Man, I've always loved them."

I open the door and let him inside. I don't think low-slung German sports cars were built for a man of Joseph's size. "Don't drool, please. He's sensitive."

Finally, I get him out of the car, and we head to my house. I take him back to the station in the Beast. He loves it.

"You know Bob, since neither of us has a wife waiting at home with a hot meal, you want to grab a bite to eat?"

"Sure, why not. We're going to work together, so we need to get to know each other."

We go to a Mexican restaurant that is a favorite of his. Good, I love Mexican food. He orders a Mexican beer, and so do I.

"Some Indians have a problem with booze as you may know. I pace myself. Two beers when out; that's it. I have had to fight too many of my own people when they were drunk out of their gourds. Not pretty. Besides, I want to keep my job."

"I respect that."

We begin to get to know each other. Joseph was born on the reservation and his mother still lives there. He has a sister who works for the Federal Bureau of Indian Affairs in Washington D.C. His dad died in Viet Nam; he was Special Forces. How many Native Americans died in service of the country that didn't want them in the first place, and stuck them in bare patches of unusable land? Kind of a sad, mind-numbing thought. But we are here to get to know each other, not discuss our ancestors.

I tell Joseph of my past; I was also in Viet Nam but not doing anything as famous as Special Forces. My personal life, my police history, and I also mention the trucker case.

"I heard about the case. I saw the flyers with your name as the contact for information. How's it coming?"

I fill him in on what I know to date and the fact the new Chief of Investigations in Santa Clara County does not want the case followed up.

"Why no follow-up?" he asks.

I tell him what Broderick said about her being a whore and asking for it.

"Man, that's just wrong." Joseph is indignant. "She was somebody's daughter and who is he to say what she was or anything about her. She was a victim and deserves to be given justice."

Joseph, you and I are going to do well together; we think alike.

"You know," Joseph says almost conspiratorially, "there are an awful lot of trucks going through here. We can always find some extra time to check out some of them, you know, when we have a moment." He winks.

I have found a partner. Evildoers, you are on

notice: your days are numbered.

We part, and true to his word, Joseph had only two beers.

The following weeks are filled with typical detective work. Big cases, little cases, and everything in between. I'm learning the county and who's who. Joseph is no Charlie, but he does know the good, the bad, and the ugly of Elko County. George is always checking in and offering his advice. He is almost as good as Charlie.

Speaking of Charlie, I receive at least one phone call a week from him. He wants to know what I'm doing, what my cases are, and how I'm handling them.

"I thought my training was done years ago," I protest good-naturedly to him one day.

"Ah, butterfly, you have learned well but still have much to master." Then he bursts out in laughter. "You kept spewing all that Karate Kid stuff, so I finally bought the movie and watched it. Mr. Mayagi was one smart cookie, much like me. Too bad I didn't think to have you wax my car."

"Good night, Charlie; I have to work tomorrow."

No sooner do I hang up than the phone rings. It's the sheriff's office dispatch. There has been a shooting and patrol wants investigation out at the scene. Since there are only two detectives that means me, and since I must go, so does Joseph. It's only fair. I tell dispatch to roust his butt and have him meet me at the scene.

The scene is a county road at the entrance to one of the local Indian reservations. Our patrol officers are there and so are the tribal police. The victim is dead. A male in his forties, and a resident of the reservation. He has been shot twice, once in the stomach and once in the back. He is lying face down, just outside the entrance to the reservation. His feet are faced toward the reservation. Patrol thinks he was running away from the shooter, since he is face down, and shot in the back. The tribal police say he was backing away from his shooter, trying to get back into the rez. The gunshot wound to the stomach being their justification. Clearly this is a "not my jurisdiction" argument. I side with patrol agreeing it is not their jurisdiction. But the same coroner will examine the body, no matter whose jurisdiction it is, and I am the detective on the scene. Patrol has taken photos, and Joseph and I take some more.

I want to go onto the reservation land and look at the area inside. Joseph knows the tribal guys and suggests we go chat with them. As Joseph chats, I begin to wander around the area inside the rez. When one of the officers starts to say something to me, Joseph starts talking to him to divert his attention. I see tire tracks in the dirt roadway that seem to be deeper than any others in the area. It looks like someone "dug out" while backing up, turned around, and went farther into the reservation. While Joseph takes the officers over to the body to discuss the wounds with them, I take my camera and shoot several quick shots of the tire tracks, then head back to Joseph. The tribal guys are getting agitated because I took pictures.

I tell them "I'm just trying to learn more about the area."

"Give me the pictures," says one of the tribal officers, making a grab for my camera.

"I'll give you a copy if they come out; it's dark, you know." He starts to get pushy, but Joseph reminds him he's now on *our* land, and it would be wise to simply tell his supervisor.

Ah, jurisdictional boundaries. I know there's a need for them but look at the problems they cause.

The coroner has taken the body so we can finally leave. I tell Joseph breakfast is on me. He knew what I wanted to do, and he helped me do it. Yes. I got me a partner.

The next afternoon I'm at my desk and in walks FBI Andy. "What the hell are you doing here? Vacation? No. You're wearing your I'm on duty' face."

He laughs and shakes my hand. "Actually, you're the reason I'm here. I want to see the photos you took last night."

"Oh god, I can see the headlines now...Lieutenant Carson arrested by FBI for taking unauthorized pictures on federal land."

Andy gets serious. "No, I want to thank you for taking them because those idiots would have driven over the tire tracks and not even noticed. I believe the shooting took place inside the reservation and you may have the only proof so far."

"Seriously?"

"Seriously."

"So why are you here? Is your staffing so thin you come from San Jose to Elko for cases?"

"I transferred to the Reno District. Just made the move and I'm looking for a house for the family, something in a rural area, real small town. I was going to call you, but this came up last night, so I decided I'd see you in person."

I ask why the Reno area and Andy says he wants a better environment than San Jose to raise his daughters.

Big cities are a tough place to raise kids. We talk while I wait for the photos to be brought to me from the lab. When they arrive, Andy is quite pleased with them.

"These are great. Why is your radio lying there? Oh, for size reference. Forgive me; it was a long drive."

"I didn't have my Official Issue FBI Ruler to lay down, so I improvised."

"I love your humor. I wish it was a requirement for our agents. Sadly, I think applicants get marked down for it."

According to Andy, a disturbance involving the shooting victim occurred in one of the houses on the reservation last night. It was broken up by the tribal police. An hour or so later, the victim is found dead just outside the reservation on the county roadway. Andy says the FBI usually does not get involved with off-reservation incidents. But since I caused a stir with my photography, the tribal police chief called the Bureau of Indian Affairs to complain of my transgression. Andy gets sent out and after hearing of the prior disturbance and looking at the house involved, which happens to have a few bullet holes, he decides there might be more to this case than the locals want to admit.

I call Joseph to come to my office so I can introduce him to Andy. When he walks in, they both chuckle and shake hands. They know each other. Okay, so how's this? *Andy just gets to the area and already knows my partner?*

A few years back, Andy was sent to Elko for a case at the reservation where Joseph was a tribal officer.

"We were short of agents and I was sent to help the Reno office. Joseph was the only officer who helped me on the case. He told me who was who and basically solved the case for me. You have a good partner here."

"Stop it, Andy. The buttons on his shirt are going to pop off. But you're correct. Joseph is an asset. He's the only reason I got those photos."

Andy will take over the shooting case, which is fine with me.

"You're sure you don't mind the FBI taking this case from you?" Andy asks. "I know how touchy you *locals* are."

"Please, I insist."

Chapter 21

Andy works his shooting case and eventually gets his man, or in this case, woman. Seems the victim's girlfriend did not approve of him seeing his wife occasionally and had it out with him. This was after the tribal police had been to the wife's house for the disturbance call, which was the wife and girlfriend fighting. The dummy went to the girlfriend's house later and they got into it. He ran down the road and she was so mad she got in her truck and chased him to the gate, where she shot him in the stomach and as he spun around, she shot him in the back. He managed to fall face first onto the dirt road. They were her tire tracks I'd photographed. Good work, FBI; I'm proud to know you.

A few days after that all settled down, I get a three-thirty a.m. phone call from dispatch. A body has been found on the shoulder of Interstate Highway 80 just outside of town. It's my case, not the city PD. I bet they found the body and dragged it over the city limit lines. Just kidding, but sometimes you wonder.

Joseph and I meet at the scene. Already there is one of our patrol units, the highway patrol, an ambulance, a fire truck, and of course the Elko PD. I hate being late to a party.

Highway patrol had received the call from a motorist traveling on the freeway who reported seeing a man and woman fighting on the other side of the roadway. They were illuminated by the headlights of a truck parked behind them. The motorist said he saw the man hit the female. He continued to the next off-ramp and called 911 from a pay phone.

He sounded quite upset as he described what he saw. He was afraid for the woman. Then the man hung up. The dispatcher sent an officer to the pay phone, the parking lot of a closed gas station. No one was around when the officer arrived. For whatever reason, the motorist did not want to stick around and talk to the police.

The officer who arrived at the scene first found a woman in her thirties lying on the side of the road. There was no truck. The woman was dead. Her throat slashed.

The female's body shows signs of facial bruising and her clothes are torn. Blood covers her upper torso and splatters the ground around her, all from the huge gash across her throat. I look closer and find she has what appears to be blood and maybe flesh under the fingernails of her right hand. She may have gotten a few licks in herself while fighting for her life. The lab will have to test to see if it is someone else's blood.

We finish the initial examination of her body and then let the coroner remove it. The other emergency responders have gone by now and it's just Joseph and me. We take photos of the entire area and closely examine the roadway and surrounding shoulder for anything that could be a clue. There is a full moon and the area is well lit. I tell Joseph we need to recheck the area again as this is our last chance to find anything while the scene is still secured. Then Joseph gets a strange look on his face and walks farther down the shoulder. He looks up at the moon and then down.

"Come here. We're missing something. I feel something here." He waves his hand toward the side of the roadway.

Here I am on the basically deserted highway with my new partner, who now is acting weird and waving at the darkness.

"I know you don't drink much, but how about peyote?"

"No. Sometimes I get feelings. That's how I solved your friend Andy's case."

I shine my flashlight around the area he is pointing toward and walk down the shoulder of the highway to the drainage ditch at the bottom.

"Keep going," he insists.

I look back at Joseph; he is still standing where I left him, still pointing in my direction.

I've read Tony Hillerman's books about shamans and medicine men, etc., but this is a kid in Elko, not a gray-haired seer from New Mexico.

I shine my light around the ditch and something flashes. I go over and it is—what the hell—it looks like an eyeball. I lean down and it sure looks like an eyeball...with blood on it. I get a cold chill. An eyeball? Come on. What would a real eyeball be doing here? Then it hits me. The victim had blood and flesh under her fingernails. Had she managed to gouge her assailant's eye out?

"Joseph, get down here." I'm not sure if I want a witness or just company.

"Is that what I think it is?" he asks with his hand over his mouth.

"I think so; turn your head away if you're going to get sick."

We get an evidence bag and, using gloves, I carefully pick up the eye and place it in the bag. We must be quite a sight. Joseph holding the evidence bag shaking so much I can hardly get the eye inside. To be completely honest I am not doing too well either. I've seen a lot of trauma in my careers of ambulance work, police work, and war but this is a *real* eyeball. Wait a moment, it's hard, not soft like a real eyeball. What is it? It has fresh blood on it. Is it a false eye? I've never encountered one before.

We finish searching the ditch and find nothing more of value. Climbing back up to the shoulder we shine our flashlights all up and down the area for the umpteenth time. I spot something lying in some weeds. It's a pair of glasses with black plastic frames. We bag them, too. After taking the evidence back to the office neither one of us is interested in breakfast; we just sit in the office try to make sense of the case.

"Okay, so what was the waving around all about?" I ask finally.

"My grandfather was a medicine man. He taught me some of the ancient ways. Sometimes I get 'feelings' about things. Like when I was drawn to walk farther down the shoulder." Joseph points through the window at the night sky. "I looked at the moon and saw an owl dive down toward that area of the ditch. I knew it was a sign. Owls are sacred to some Native Americans, they are symbols of wisdom and intuition. They see through the darkness, which is symbolic of ignorance and discern the path free from distraction. Some tribes find owls to be frightening. I have always been drawn to them. Guess it paid off, huh?" He softly smiles, the light from the moon highlighting his sturdy features.

I sit there contemplating it all.

"Joseph, I want you to always be my partner as long as you're here. I may not understand all of this, but I'm impressed."

"I'm not going anywhere, Boss."

"Seriously, you have a good mind for investigation and this extra talent of yours will make you even better. You also need to think of your future. You could go far in this business."

"My home is here. My mom lives here, and I want to be near her. I like it at the sheriff's office, especially since you came along. I'm your boy, Lieutenant."

"Bob; I told you to call me Bob."

"Right, Lieutenant." He laughs at me.

The next day the lab examines the eyeball. It is a prosthetic eye fitted to a person who has lost their own eye due to trauma or disease. They get the blood type from it and it is not from the victim. It is the same type as the blood under her fingernails.

The glasses are not prescription, just plastic lenses. Maybe a connection to the eye? A disguise of some type?

Now we're getting somewhere. She wounded her killer. We start to build our case with the facts we know. He appears to have only one eye, for now anyway. He can probably get a new artificial replacement soon. He drives a truck. Wait a minute...a truck driver who kills women. No, can't be, can it? I may be on "my case" again. What is with the artificial eye? I don't know what to make of this.

Unfortunately, the only witness is the missing motorist. I'm going to ask the media to issue a plea for him to get in touch with me. Slim chance, but worth the effort. He could be local or on his way east to Utah or north to Idaho or wherever. Elko is a major crossroads for travelers. I listen to the 911 tape from his call. He says he saw a man and woman fighting in front of a truck. No mention of the size of the truck. I can only assume it was a large commercial truck. If it had been a pickup truck, the witness might not have been able to tell if it was a pickup or a car from across the highway. I know I'm grasping here.

The victim is identified later in the day. She lived in Wells, Nevada, a small town about an hour's drive east of Elko. Joseph and I drive to Wells. It's at the intersection of I-80 and US Highway 93. This is a major North-South and East-West crossroads, but there is not much here. A couple of truck stops, gas stations, convenience markets, fast food chains, and a few bars. And being Nevada there's a casino and some houses of ill repute.

Prostitution is legal in eight counties of Nevada, including Elko and Wells. Regular people live here, too. There is hunting, fishing, and beautiful mountains nearby. Possibly some connection between the hunting and fishing and the aforementioned houses, but I'm not sure what. Maybe outdoorsmen need something else to do at night. Speculation on my part. The sheriff's office does not get many calls to these places. No one seems to want to make any official reports.

Since there is no police department in Wells, the sheriff's office has a sub-station located here. Joseph and I meet with the resident deputy. "The victim's parents called the sheriff's office when they realized she didn't return home last night."

"A woman in her thirties still living at home?"

"She's a local grade school teacher. Housing options are limited in Wells. Her parents run a grocery store and have for years. She helped in the store when needed, even though she worked full-time as a teacher."

The parents have already been notified of their daughter's death. We go with the deputy to meet them at the store; as expected, they are emotional, especially the mother. She says her husband wanted her to stay home, but she had to come to the store. She needs to stay busy and does not want to be alone. By now everyone in Wells knows of the death. Residents have been coming in all day long, giving their condolences to the couple.

Choking back tears, the father says, "Our daughter, Dorothy, worked in the store last night from five p.m. until closing at nine p.m. This was so my wife and I could go to dinner with some friends who were celebrating their anniversary. After dinner, we went home to bed. We open the store early. It wasn't until this morning we realized Dorothy had not come home at all. We talked with her just before she closed the store and she said she would be home later. It's not unusual. She has friends in town."

With all the people who came to the store with condolences, no one mentioned seeing Dorothy last night. The deputy had already gone to the local bars and casino to ask if anyone had seen her. He plans to go back when the swing shift crew comes on duty.

"Any chance of video tapes in any of these spots?" I'm hoping for a visual on the girl and whoever she might have been with.

"There are some, I'm sure of that."

I ask him to check them out with his night deputy who will come on duty shortly. They both knew the victim and will recognize her.

Joseph and I get back in our car. "Any feelings?" I ask.

He stares through the windshield for a minute. "No, they don't come all the time you know, just sometimes. Nothing right now, maybe later."

The parents give us the names of some of their daughter's friends, so we start to locate them. Now it is after six in the evening. We find one person home who is a fellow teacher. She has already heard the news and is drowning her sorrows with white wine. She had not seen Dorothy since school yesterday. Knew she was going to work the store for her parents. Gives us some more names and offers to call everyone over to talk to us. Sounds like a plan. Soon we have four female and one male teacher talking with us. None had seen her since school yesterday. They all agree Dorothy was a good girl who did not party. She would drink a little but never to excess. She did not gamble.

Then the resident deputy calls me on my cell and informs me he has Dorothy on a surveillance tape at the casino. We thank everyone for their cooperation and leave for the casino.

The deputy takes us to the casino's surveillance room, which is basically a closet with recorders. Picture this: three cops and the casino security guy, all crammed in trying to see the tiny screen. The tape shows Dorothy with a white male at the bar around nine-thirty p.m. last night. As I strain to look at the male, I get a weird sensation. It's *Weaton*. I swear it is. I am suddenly looking into the face of the murderer I have been chasing for so many years.

Joseph glances at me. "It's him, isn't it?"

No hooded sweatshirt, and now his head is shaved. He has a mustache, dark in color. He's wearing glasses with dark frames. It's him. I know it is. I am overcome with emotion finally seeing him. Of course, I don't show it. But then Joseph puts his bear paw of a hand on my shoulder and gives it a squeeze. That does it. I need to back out of the room and take a deep breath.

"Okay, is there anything more?" I ask in my most controlled voice.

As the security officer scrolls the tape forward in time, we watch the couple drink two rounds, then leave. Dorothy seems to be drinking wine and Weaton/Colter—whichever he is—beer. He pays with cash. The security officer scans more locations and finds they went to dinner in the coffee shop. Again, he pays with cash. The coffee shop cameras only watch the cash registers. About 11:15 p.m. they leave the coffee shop. There are no outside cameras, so this is it. We then go to the bartender. He had seen her before and knew she was a local who came in with her girlfriends now and then. Never a problem, a couple drinks, that was all. The waitress from the coffee shop said the couple appeared to be "getting to know" each other. She thought they were getting cozier by the end of the meal. They were holding hands when they left.

We leave the casino, taking the video with us. I thank the deputy.

Joseph heads to the driver's door of our vehicle. "I'll drive," he says kindly.

"Good idea, thanks." I climb in the passenger side and sink into the seat.

Joseph starts up the car. "We're going to the truck stops. He has to park his rig somewhere."

The boy is on it.

There are two main truck stops and several places where truckers park around the crossroads. We split up and begin to ask anyone we see about Weaton/Colton and Dorothy. Alone or together. We have the flyers I keep in my police vehicle and show them his pictures. We also have a recent photo of Dorothy her parents gave us. No one can help. A couple of people remember a man and woman walking toward some parked trucks around midnight, but that's about it.

We're exhausted and hungry. We go back to the casino coffee shop to eat before the drive back to Elko. The same waitress is still on duty. She comes over. "I've been trying to rack my brain to think of anything that could help out. I am fairly sure she called him Dave. If that means anything."

That means everything. He's still using David Allen Colton's ID. That's what it means.

We thank her and ask her to call if she thinks of anything else. I show her the flyer on the two identities, Weaton and Colton. She looked closely and gasps. "I knew I remembered that voice. He has been in here before, several times. He looks like that fellow there. But he called himself Al." She points to Weaton's photos on the flyer.

"He used to stop in all the time. I loved his voice. It was so smooth, and you know, syrupy. A real southern gentleman's accent. Then he didn't come in anymore."

"Do you remember when he stopped coming in?" I

ask.

She thinks about it. "At least a year or two. He was really sweet to me. I'm a little bit older than him, but he kept trying to get me to hang around after shift and have a drink with him. I told him, 'Honey, you're a real cutie, but I got my own cutie at home and that's where I'm going. Thank you anyway.'"

Then she studies the rest of the flyer. "He's wanted for murder before this time?" She turns pale and sits down next to me.

"He's a real charmer, huh?"

"First class," she says. "You know, now that I think about it, he didn't look at me very much last night and kind of mumbled his order. But I could hear him talking to that poor girl and he was as sweet as ever. You need to get him."

I do not say it, but I'm sure she realizes that by being true to her man, she probably saved her life.

Chapter 22

Can't sleep. I'm beat but my mind won't shut down. It's racing over everything I know about Weaton/Colton. Finally, I pour myself a large Crown Royal and manage to drift off.

When I walk into the office the next morning Joseph is already working the phones.

"Hi Bob, I've been calling all the hospitals and clinics between here and Reno to see if he went in for his wounds. No luck so far."

"How long have you been here?"

"A couple of hours. I couldn't sleep."

"Me either."

We sit down and work out a plan of action. Then I update George and the sheriff. They're blown away at how much we already know. I hadn't told anyone except Joseph about "my case" so it is all new to them. They knew I had a suspect I was trailing, but they didn't know my personal connection. The retelling hurt almost as much as the original discovery. Things like this never seem to ease in a person's mind. They stay fresh. Bright pictures that never fade.

I want to make new flyers with the latest photo from the surveillance tapes and add it to the older ones. The sheriff says he knows a local artist who can make a good picture of Weaton from the tapes. This is great because video tapes are never truly clear.

"How can he be a trucker with one eye?" asks George. "He couldn't get his CDL."

It dawns on me. "He had one eye and wanted to keep being a truck driver. That's why he became Colton. He needed to find someone he could pass as and a person who already had a CDL. So when did he lose his eye? I remember, *damn I hate getting older*; I should have thought of it before. Gloria, Weaton's ex-wife in Enid, Oklahoma, told me she met him in the hospital where she worked. He had been injured. The two sisters I interviewed (the high school kid and her "dumb" sister) both mentioned his face being distorted on the right side.

I call Greg from Enid PD on his cell and ask him to question Gloria about the injury. "Here, you can ask her yourself."

Gloria comes on the line. I knew he was being more than "professionally concerned" with her.

"Bill had his right eye torn out when a binding chain broke on his truck. His cheek bone was broken and reset. He lost the eye and had to get a false one."

"When did this happened?" I ask.

She is able to give me a date. Then I want to know when he was out of the hospital and back on the road. She says he went back driving within a couple of weeks.

"What about the eye?"

"He started back driving wearing a patch. He needed the money for this truck payment he said. He got the false eye later."

Checking her time frame with "my case," he is still good for it. He was back on the road then.

I don't know what, if anything, I can do with the

eye, but it is evidence. Is it possible to link it to Weaton? I ask George about local eye doctors and he tells me to go see his. He's been around for years.

I meet with the doctor and show him the eye.

He explains, "I don't make eyes; that's done by an ocularist. There aren't many, especially in Nevada. I know of one in Reno, and I have sent a couple of patients to him."

I get the name and phone number: P.K. Kelly. I need to go to Reno. I can hook up with Mike from Reno P.D. and have a change of pace for one day.

Oh shit, I forgot. Snow. I have now been exposed to the nasty white stuff and extreme cold weather. I will need to drive for endless hours in bad weather. Maybe I can wait until the forecast is better, like springtime. No, I need to do this right now. I check and find out the present weather pattern is due to break and next week will be better. Whatever that means.

I place a call to P.K. Kelly and a very pleasant receptionist answers. I identify myself and ask if I can make an appointment with Mr. Kelly and show him my evidence for his professional opinion.

She says, "I'm sure he'll be happy to help. When would you like to come in? You're from Elko. That's not a nice drive this time of year."

We set a date for the next Tuesday. Since I'm driving from Elko, the appointment will be later in the afternoon. She says that will be fine, Mr. Kelly will wait for me.

"Be careful on the road," she adds. Cheerful voice; sweet too. Probably married to Mr. Kelly. Well, maybe not, I'll just have to see. The dating scene has been skimpy here in Elko. Between the long hours, added to the fact I have two left feet, and neither one of them can master the two-step, I have been limited. Nothing against country music, but around here, the Eagles are birds that fly in the Ruby Mountains. I've got to talk with George and the sheriff. I need another detective...soon.

Time to recheck the national data centers for anything on Weaton or Colton. The CDL for Colton is getting close to renewal. *Has it been that long?* I guess it has. I placed the Santa Clara County murder warrant into the system a long time ago, with no response. Checking, it is still there under both names and SSNs and dates of birth. Now our county attorney has issued a murder warrant for Weaton/Colton. I ask the county dispatch supervisor to also start regular checks on the two. Being the lieutenant, I no longer rely on donuts and candy, I can just ask. Nice, but I still bring around goodies every so often.

Later in the day one of the dispatchers calls me. "Lieutenant, I may have found your man Colton...at least a month ago. He may have been in one of about thirty vehicles involved in a huge accident in a snowstorm in the Midwest."

"Great, can you get me any kind of a report?"

"I'll try. It was in Kansas. Hopefully, they're finished with the report by now. I looked the accident up on the internet. It was a mess."

I can only hope it will have the name of the trucking company on the report. That will confirm he is still Colton.

Later the dispatcher calls back. "I spoke to the Kansas Highway Patrol. The records guy laughed when I asked about a report. If the person didn't go to the hospital, then no real report is completed. They take down the names of anyone involved and tell them to get moving. He gave his name as David Colton. I guess Kansas HP only asks for a driver's license; they don't write down anything but the name. For insurance purposes, he said. No addresses, no employers, license numbers, nothing. If a tow truck is needed, then they will note that. Colton apparently did not need a tow. Sorry, lieutenant, I tried."

I thank her for the quick work. I guess if you have that many vehicles involved in the middle of a blizzard, you just do what you can to get it cleared up. Could that happen here? Don't want to think about it.

He was a name on a report. Did not trip the "hit" button in the system. Probably was Weaton/Colton but it doesn't matter. I have nothing to go on. With his CDL expiring soon, he may find another "Colton" and assume his identity.

Some time ago George initiated a monthly meeting of investigators along Interstate 80. Since much of our area is sparsely populated and the local "bad boys" must travel to keep busy, it seemed like a good idea. It has solved more than a few cases. The next meeting will be after I get back from Reno. I fax my new flyers to the other agencies. I even call FBI Andy and fill him in. Yes, I tell the enemy.

I call Mike Harper at Reno P.D. and tell him I'll be coming to his town on Tuesday.

"Great," he says. "We can go to dinner and you can meet my new girlfriend."

He's got a girlfriend, when is it my turn?

The Monday before I am to leave for Reno I make a final check with the dispatchers. Nothing new on my search for Weaton/Colton.

As I put down the phone, I see a very well-dressed Native American lady walk past my office. Then I hear Joseph's voice. "Hey, Sis. What are you doing here? Why didn't you tell me you were coming?" There's animated conversation and then he says, "Come and meet my boss."

Into my office comes Joseph and his sister. "Lieutenant, I want you to meet my *older* sister, Mary."

She gives him a look. "I'm so glad to meet you. Joseph has told me so much about you. I want to thank you for looking after him. He needs guidance sometimes." She smiles as she pokes at him.

I tell her I am pleased to meet her, and Joseph is a great detective. I'm proud to have him as a partner.

"So, I understand you're with the BIA. How do you like Washington?"

"Well, the reason I'm here; we received a complaint you were violating sacred land by taking pictures." She looks stone-faced at me, then breaks out into laughter. "I'm sorry, but Joseph told me about the idiot tribal police incident, and I just had to tease you. Good job. The FBI report to us also complimented your actions as being the reason they solved the shooting."

"I see Joseph isn't the only one in his family with humor."

She says the real reason she's here is to introduce a new area administrator to the local reservations. She looks at Joseph and declares, "You'll be at dinner tonight at Mom's, right?" He nods and she leaves.

"Older sister?"

"Yeah, she is but doesn't like me saying it. That's why I do." He grins.

After work I get ready for my big trip to Reno. The weather looks good. I'll have my county 4-wheel drive vehicle so I should be okay. I still haven't gotten used to the cold and ice and that white stuff.

Chapter 23

The next morning, I stop by the office, go over cases with Joseph, and check on the weather again. Still looking good.

"Did you make it to Mom's last night like you were told, Joseph?"

"Yes, Dad, I did. Now tonight I must have dinner with my sister and the new BIA person. Why do I have to go? I don't have to work with him. No big deal."

"But you'll be there, right?"

"Yes, Dad. Better get on the road. I'm not sure about the weather holding."

"Is that an Indian thing or did you look at the forecast?"

"Indian thing. Get on the road, Boss." He grins.

Long drive, four hours normally even with *my-get-out-of-jail-free* card, my badge. But my personal shaman was right. About halfway, I start to get some snow. The usual seventy-plus speed is not going to happen today.

I slow down and let my mind wander. I'm getting my hopes up again about "my case." Could this be a real clue to it? The case is never far from my consciousness. Every truck is a reminder. How many have I watched? How many drivers have I unnerved by slowing down and staring at them?

It's four in the afternoon when I finally get to Reno

and I'm cranky and tired. I hope Mr. Kelly is still here. I find the office. It is in a modest medical building close to a hospital. On the door is a sign:

P.K. Kelly
Ocularist

I walk into the small waiting area. A receptionist is seated at a desk in front of a door I assume leads to the "eye guy's" office. The receptionist is attractive, petite, shoulder length blonde hair, professionally dressed, younger than I, but not too much. Just a "personal observation by a trained observer." I would say she is the same person I spoke to on the phone.

She greets me courteously. I identify myself and ask for the "eye guy." Smiling slightly, she says, "Oh yes, he's expecting you. I'll tell him you're here." She leaves through the door behind her desk. I hope the pretty woman comes back before I leave, because I would like to talk to her...and not about the case. Noticed there's no wedding ring. Again, the trained observer. At least she is not married to Mr. Kelly.

After about two minutes the door opens, and she comes out wearing a white lab coat with the name P.K. Kelly Ocularist embroidered on it.

"Hi, I'm the eye guy," she says.

Stumbling in my most humble manner I say, "I'm sorry...I thought with the name...uhh...well, you know I just thought...uhh," or something brilliant like that.

She rescues me with a smile. "It's alright, a number of people make that assumption, even some of the doctors who refer patients to me."

Trying to regain some composure I say, "Well, it was still wrong to *assume* it could only be only a man, especially in this day and age."

"That's how it is...still. Now, you mentioned a prosthetic eye on the phone."

I reach into my coat pocket and bring out the eye in a plastic evidence bag. Holding it out to her I ask, "Can you tell me anything about this?"

"May I open the bag and examine the eye?"

"Oh yeah, sure, if you want...uh...need to," I stammer.

Looking at me with her beautiful brown eyes she says, "If you want me to tell you anything other than it's an artificial eye, then yes, I'll need to examine it."

She takes the bag from me, opens it, and gently removes the prothesis. She looks at it with an art critic's discerning eye—pun intended—rotating it and seeming to peer into it. After a few quiet minutes she announces, "It was made by an ocularist in San Antonio, Texas."

Hoping my mouth isn't gaping open, I ask, "How do you know that?"

"We all leave a mark on our work. Like an artist signing a painting. However, I don't know what this scratching is on the back. Looks like a cattle brand or something."

Puffing my chest out, I reply, "That is *my* mark. We also mark our work or in this case, evidence. That's so I can state in court, *this* is the same item I found at the crime scene."

She looks at me with those eyes again and I'm sure there is a smile in there saying, *oh okay*.

Now the chest is back to normal. This lady is tough, obviously not easily impressed. Well, back to the case.

P.K. Kelly proceeds to talk about the eye, informing me it is a right eye and from an adult. Since it is blue, chances are it belongs to a Caucasian. No guarantee. Then she looks at me and seems to expect a response.

I'm mesmerized by it all—her eyes, demeanor, professional knowledge, but mainly her eyes. Suddenly, I realize I'm supposed to say something.

"I'm impressed. You hold it like a mother with a child, gentle, caring. It's like you feel a kinship with it."

She smiles. "My turn. You do get it. I'm impressed. Don't let it go to your head, though."

She's on to me. "How do you know it was made in San Antonio? Is there a brand registry, like cattle?"

I get that look again; oops.

"No, I went to school with the lady who uses this mark."

Not one to give up easily, I ask more questions and get a lot of information. I did not know these things were hand-painted to match the remaining eye. Most of this knowledge will not help me but it keeps her talking.

Time to get serious. "I drove straight through from Elko and I'm hungry. Would you have a restaurant you could recommend for dinner? A nice place, one you like."

"I suppose you're a steak and potatoes man?"

"No, I enjoy a varied cuisine." I'm not lying. I like most food but raw fish, liver, or any place smelling of lamb are my absolute avoid eateries.

"Well, there's a nice Italian place I frequent that's especially good," she replies, very businesslike. No hint there. I go for it.

"Since I started out so badly would you let me buy you dinner?" I stop breathing, waiting for an answer.

She's thinking...I see a hint of a smile or hope I do.

"Sure," she says. "I'll meet you there at seven."

I start to breathe again. "Would you give me the address?" I give my best smile.

She does and a happy cop leaves for his hotel to clean up. I call Mike Harper and tell him I must cancel as I have a date.

"Good for you. Want to join us or probably not?"

"Probably not. Maybe next time, if there is one."

I check into my room and take a quick shower. Cleaned up and presentable, sport coat, open neck shirt, and khakis, casual, not overdone, I depart for my date.

Arriving at the restaurant, I realize it is the same one Harper took me to. I also remember this is an upscale joint. Happy my credit cards are still in good shape.

I am immediately met by the same large, well-dressed maître d' as last time. He is soft spoken and asks if I have a reservation. I tell him I am waiting for someone and will be in the bar.

"What is the name of the party?" he asks. Runs a tight ship, I like that.

"P.K. Kelly," I say.

He gives me a strong once-over and says efficiently, somewhat coolly, "When she arrives, I will tell her you're here."

What's that about? Is the big guy competition or just looking out for a good customer? I never did like maître d's.

I order my usual Tanqueray and tonic with a lime. I sip. I don't want to be looking the fool when she arrives. I'm nervous. I like her and I am impressed with her knowledge and her beauty, eyes, etc. I want to get to know her better.

When she comes in the front door, the ass of a host, okay, the maître d', immediately goes up to her and throws his arms around her. He lifts her off the ground in a bear hug. He's big and she's petite. Then he puts her down. I take one more sip.

The big jerk points to me dismissively and she comes over to me. I stand up, not sure what to do next.

"Mind if I join you?" Again, with that captivating smile.

"Please do." Always the gentleman, I turn the bar stool next to me.

She hops up and asks, "What are you having?"

"Tanqueray and tonic."

"Ugh, gin. How do you stand it? Like lighter fluid."

The bartender comes right over to her. "Hey, P.K. haven't seen you in a while. What are you drinking?"

"I think a Bloody Mary, please."

She turns to me. "Have any trouble finding this place?"

I tell her I have been here before with a Reno police officer. "You seem known here. The big guy was sure happy to see you. Quite a greeting."

"That's my brother. Same mother, different father."

No wonder he was checking me out.

We start chatting. We seem to be genuinely hitting it off. We sit there sipping and talking. The bartender leaves us alone. Finally, I realize she's finished her drink and I ask if she would like another. We both get another round and keep talking. It's like we have been together before. Just so easy.

Big brother comes over and asks if we are ready

for dinner. He shows us to a table. A pleasant waitress comes over and gives P.K. a hug. "This is my sister in-law," she says, introducing me.

The big guy's wife. Boy is P.K. safe in this place. This lady is on it. She knows where to take her first dates.

We order dinner and honestly, I don't remember much about the food. It's good, but we keep talking, about every subject it seems.

We get around to the eye. She wants to know the story behind it. I tell her it was found at the scene of a murder.

"Blue eyes are very difficult to match properly." She goes on to tell me how she creates the eyes and what is involved with the coloring of the iris. She paints layers of color on the surface of a disk of x-ray film, which is placed in the finished replacement eye. She needs to adjust the finished prosthetic to work with the remaining eye muscles, so the artificial eye appears to move naturally. She's an artist and a mechanical engineer; impressive. What a talented lady and I'm getting along with her. More importantly, she is getting along with me.

P.K. also does paintings, real artsy stuff. Pastels, oils, that kind of painting, and she's still talking with me.

She asks me more about the murder. I tell her the story about Weaton/Colton.

She gets a strange look on her lovely face. "When did this happen?"

"A week ago. Tuesday night, early Wednesday morning."

"I received a phone call late Wednesday afternoon.

It was from a man with a southern accent, who had just lost his prosthetic eye. He wanted to know how fast I could make him a new eye. When I told him it would take three days, he became agitated, said he couldn't stay that long. When I asked him why, he told me he was a truck driver and had to make a delivery in California. I asked if he could come back after he made the delivery, and he said he had to pick up another load and go south. I mentioned he might go to the ocularist who made the first one. He said he didn't know when he would be in Texas again."

P.K. looks at me. "That was him, wasn't it?"

"Most likely, but he's gone now. I assume you are in the phone book and internet, and he found your name. He probably called from a truck stop."

It frightens me she had contact with this guy. In fact, it makes my stomach knot up. I reach over and touch her hand. She puts her other hand on mine, and we stay that way for a few minutes.

Dessert is finished and we're sipping the last of our wine when P.K. looks at me, her eyes softening, "I possibly shouldn't tell you this, but I have enjoyed your company. I genuinely have. You seem so easy to talk with, like we've known each other forever."

"I totally agree. I'm relaxed with you. Why shouldn't you tell me that?"

She shyly looks down at the wine glass and then back at me. "You live on the other side of the world, but I'd like to see you again."

I could jump up, do handsprings, run around the room, and kiss the big guy. I am blown away.

"You know I feel the same, and Elko is not *that* far away. I have time on the books; there are weekends.

We can do this."

"You mean it? I would like to take things slowly, see where it leads us. Know what I mean? I like you, Robert."

She seems to like calling me Robert. Fine with me as long as she keeps talking.

"I told you about my life and you've told me about yours. So," she smiles warmly, "let's give it a try. Okay?"

"Okay, P.K. I'm in." I smile back. Wait, I do not smile much, but I did. I know I did.

We keep talking until it becomes obvious we're the only diners still left in the restaurant. No one has bothered us, but it's a weeknight and they will want to close soon.

I leave with her home phone number and she stays to talk with big brother, who smiles and shakes my hand when I leave. This is a good start, hell it's a great start. Reno, Elko, like next door. I'll be back, often...I hope.

Chapter 24

Early the next morning I head back to Elko. I'm floating and the miles fly by. I pull into the office late in the afternoon. Joseph is at his desk.

"Hey Lieutenant, how was the trip?"

"Absolutely wonderful."

"Tell me about it. This is way more than business. I can tell."

I just smile and start to walk to my office.

"Oh no, you aren't getting away that easy. Come on, give." He has his large hands held up like a stop sign. I'm not getting past him.

"All right, if you must know. The ocularist is an incredibly beautiful lady. We had dinner together and I'm going to be seeing her."

"Whoa, that's great, Boss. Now I have something to tell *you*."

"Let me guess. The dinner with the BIA person turned out to be a blind date your sister set up. Right?"

"Now how in the hell did you guess? Your powers are rivaling mine."

"Never underestimate the abilities of the white man."

"B.S. How did you know?"

"As I was leaving town for Reno yesterday, I saw your sister and a nice-looking Native American lady sitting at a stop light as I drove past. Elementary, my dear Joseph."

"Yeah, deductive reasoning, Sherlock."

He had been checking on Weaton/Colton and nothing had popped up yet. I fill him in on the phone call P.K. received from a trucker needing his prosthetic eye replaced.

"Wow, that was close, Bob. You're closing in on him."

I cannot stop clenching my fists every time I think about the call. What if she had made the appointment and he was alone with her? Disgust and fear rage through me thinking what could have happened. "It makes me nervous he came so close to P.K. She knows his background now and our suspicion he's a serial killer. I couldn't stand it if something happened to that lady."

"It is like fate brought you two together. She is protected by you and the knowledge about the trucker. You learned more about him. Places he has been, and he's getting nervous."

"Joseph, you have a way of putting things in perspective. You're so right on this."

We resume work on our other cases. Joseph takes off for one of the reservations to talk to a witness. We do not investigate crimes on the rez, but many of our cases involve residents from them. He can communicate better than I, and he is respected by most of the locals.

Honestly, I am worthless right now. My mind is still on P.K. I need to do something productive. I called her when I reached Elko, as instructed. She wanted to know I made the trip safely. The sound of her cheery voice set me off. I wanted to turn around and head back to Reno. *Settle down. You need a job, and this is a good one.* So get to work.

Any unsolved crime report from the Patrol Division will be sent to Investigations (that's Joseph and me). Part of my job is to sort them out for the ones that have something to go on: evidence, witnesses, anything we can work with. The rest of the reports just get filed. With only the two of us, a lot of cases fall into the latter category.

The patrol deputies do a great job of following up on a lot of crimes. Since they know their area, they usually have an idea of who to talk to. They help Investigations out a lot. Looking over the reports I notice one swing shift deputy has been aggressive in following up on crimes he had been assigned. Maybe he might want to become a full-time detective. Heck, a slight bump in pay and getting called out in the middle of the night, what's not to like?

I wander down to Undersheriff George's office. He thinks it's a good idea. "I admit Joseph and you need help, desperately. The staffing has improved, and some deputies are staying around after they make probation. I'm damn proud of that fact."

Don't want to burst his bubble, but maybe the other law enforcement agencies in the area have finally filled up. No, I won't say anything.

"The sheriff's office has had an open posting for the Detective I position for some time. The first one to raise his or her hand will be hired. Provided you approve."

George calls the swing shift patrol sergeant, and wouldn't you know it, the patrol deputy is working tonight. He will be dispatched to come to George's office as soon as he comes on duty. Poor guy will be sweating bullets. *"What the hell have I done now?"* I know. I have been there. The difference is, I had probably done something. Not bad, just enough to get called on the carpet.

The deputy I am interested in including in our division is Gary Horton. I get his personnel file. He has been on the department for almost two years, came from Barstow PD in California. He was there one year and had previously been on the Long Beach, PD for five years. Long Beach to Barstow...raises questions. Digging deeper I see he left Long Beach over a "use of excessive force" charge. Makes sense. Gets in trouble, goes to smaller department, which isn't too fussy or truly needs help and then gets accepted at a larger department, us. I see George did the background checking on him. He recommended hiring Horton based on talking with previous supervisors. Familiar story. Basically, a good police officer gets into trouble, tries to redeem himself in the first police job he can find, and then tries to move back into a larger agency. Why Elko? Boy from California into the waste land of eastern Nevada. Oh yeah, the hunting, fishing, etc. Well, I'll be talking with Horton and asking these questions.

I go to George again. "I did not hire Gary Horton. The sheriff and previous undersheriff conducted the interview. Horton has been a good officer and has caused no problems. You have to work with him. It's your decision if he's a good fit."

A little different than in the big city where seventeen people must sign off on anything, especially personnel matters. And usually at least three of those are on vacation and you must wait to get any decision. I'm exaggerating, but not by much.

In the meantime, I talk with Joseph who has returned from his outing. "Dinner tonight with the lady?"

He blushes.

"Caught me. Yes, I uhh...well ..." I stop him.

"Have a good date. But before you go, what's your thought on Deputy Horton?"

"Gary? He is a good guy. I was his training officer for a couple of months before George tagged me for Investigations. Gary didn't need a t.o. but he had to learn his way around and all. Good guy, why?"

"What do you think of working with him?"

"Here? That would be great with me. I always wondered why he didn't apply for Investigations, with his experience and all."

"That's one of the questions I'll be asking when he comes in later. He didn't apply; I'm recruiting him based on his reports I've read."

"You want me to hang around or anything?"

"No. Go enjoy your evening."

A few minutes after he leaves, in walks Deputy Horton. He went to George's office as instructed and was sent to me with no explanation. You can tell from the tense look on his face he's apprehensive.

He appears professional in his clean fresh uniform. Five-foot-ten or so, blue eyes, medium build, sandy blond, close cut hair. California surfer boy comes to mind. He had no warning of the meeting, so he is just as he reported for his shift. Pride in his professional appearance, I like that.

"Deputy Horton, I'm Lieutenant Carson. Please sit

down." I point to one of the chairs in front of my desk.

"Thank you, sir, I'm glad to meet you. I hear you're a California guy yourself."

I go to the office door, close it, then take the other chair in front of the desk. I have always liked it when someone will sit "with me" and not "across from me" in an interview. Horton seems to respond to this; he relaxes a little.

"I'll get right to the point, Gary. I've been reviewing the reports you've done while working patrol. I like them. You are from a larger department where you were well-trained. Your work shows that. It also shows me you want to go beyond simply taking a report. You want to dig, get all the information you can, and follow up."

"Yes sir, I have always wanted to finish any case I started. I know a patrol officer can't always do that, but I try when I can."

"You don't have to call me sir. Elko is much more casual than Long Beach. Tell me, why did you come here? I understand the move to Barstow after Long Beach, but why here? Simply curious, do you hunt or fish?"

"No, I'm probably the only one in the sheriff's office who doesn't."

"There are two; I don't either."

He laughs.

"Okay, Gary, here's the deal. I need another detective. You interested? The hours are unpredictable as we have the whole frickin' county to cover, not just a patrol beat. There is Joseph, whom I believe you know, and me."

He gets a broad smile on his face, "Yes sir, I am, I

mean Lieutenant."

"Call me Bob. Now let us go over your history so I know who and what I'm going to be working with."

"I suppose you mean Long Beach?"

I nod.

He continues. "Well, I hit this guy who had just beaten up his girlfriend. I knew her because I had dated her previously. We didn't click, but she's a nice lady. I responded to a call of a domestic disturbance. A neighbor had called 911. The guy opened the door and I saw her, face all bloody, lying on the floor of her apartment. He had a beer in his hand. He said, 'What the hell do you want, pig?' I unleashed on him. Laid him out."

"One punch?"

"No, he was big, took two."

"Did you have a backup?"

"It hadn't arrived yet. I knew it was her apartment and went right up to the door."

"In retrospect, would you handle it differently?"

"Under the same circumstances probably not. I won't lie to you, Lieutenant...Bob."

I give him an understanding nod. "I can deal with that. I appreciate your honesty. So why Barstow? First job available?"

"Pretty much. I wanted to stay on as a police officer. So yes, Barstow was the first one who was desperate enough to hire me." He smiles. "I'm glad I got right back into it. Barstow is a nice little town, but I didn't want to stay there. Too close to old memories. So I applied at a few places and Elko was the first to get interested."

"You don't hunt or fish, what do you like here?

Plan on staying?"

"I kind of found myself. Don't get worried, I'm not getting all weird, but I feel comfortable, like it's home. All I have known is big city life, but I like it here. The people are friendly. I only socialized with other cops before, you know how it is. Here I have made friends with civilians. Who knows, I might even go fishing."

We talk for a while longer. I like him. He hadn't applied for detective yet because he thought it was an "old boy's thing" and he would have to wait his turn. Gary is divorced, hence the memories from California. He doesn't have a steady girlfriend. Perfect for the job.

"Here are my rules." I tell him, "I want the job done. We both know how it can get out there. If you run into a situation that could come back on you, I want to know immediately. No surprises. I'll back you one hundred percent if you're right, and if you step on your dick I want to know before someone calls the sheriff. I cannot help if I don't know first-hand. Understood?"

"Yes sir. I appreciate it. I won't let you down."

We shake hands and I tell him I will make the arrangements to get him on board as soon as possible. He goes out on his patrol a happy cop.

Now *this* happy cop goes home to call the one who makes him a happy cop.

As soon as I hear her sweet voice, I'm in heaven. Thank goodness for cell phones and no long-distance charges. We talk until I realize the only light in my place is from the phone. She asks if I'm going to come to Reno soon and I tell her I will be there as soon as my new detective has gotten his feet wet.

"Pour some water on him; I want to see you again."

The happy cop is ecstatic.

Chapter 25

I must wait two weeks for Gary to come onboard. The patrol captain begs for more time. I feel his pain, but mine is worse. He has more manpower to draw from than I do. The investigations unit has four desks in one large room plus my office. Sadly, all four desks have never been filled. At least now there will be three of us working cases.

Joseph is a happy camper as he now has a "lady" friend and I'm still ecstatic over my good fortune. I just want to be able to get time off for at least a long weekend in Reno. I'm burning up my cell phone with the long phone calls. I cannot believe how long we can talk. Two people who have made a connection. We have barely touched physically, but emotionally I have never felt closer to anyone. I want the physical part, too. Soon.

The two weeks pass, and Gary comes to work dressed almost too nicely for our usual attire but that's okay. He's eager.

I show him around the office. Not a long tour with two rooms, but he stops at our bulletin board and looks at the flyers of Weaton/Colton and all the appearance changes I've made to them. Gary points at one of the drawings. The one where Weaton had dyed his hair black and grew the beard.

"I've seen this guy. I'm sure. It was in Barstow.

Yeah, he was a truck driver. He had a breakdown and was on the side of I-15 which runs through Barstow. I stopped to see what was going on. He had already called for assistance, so I just talked with him for a while before the service truck arrived. He was a pleasant guy. Nice southern accent. The pleasant kind, not the screechy kind some of them have."

"Do you remember when?"

"It was shortly before I came here. So it would be a little over two years ago. I never ran him for wants or even checked his license. He wasn't nervous with me, so I had no reason to. He was already wanted for murder by then?"

"I had a warrant out by then. He is probably good for two or three more murders, but you wouldn't have known back then. You would have seen the original flyer before he changed his appearance."

Gary looks at the flyers again. "I remember seeing the first one in the station. Since we were on the interstate and an east-west crossroad, we'd been sent the flyer by the FBI, I think. Dammit, we only had the first one then. So close."

"Big question, any idea of the trucking line or any personal information he gave, like where he called home, anything?"

"I'm trying to remember the truck. It was yellow. So was the trailer. BJ, yes, BJ Trucking Lines. They're always out there. You see them everywhere. Big outfit. He said something about Salt Lake City. I think that is the company headquarters. No, he didn't say anything too personal that I remember. Small talk stuff. Wait, he did like NASCAR. Big fan. Worked his schedules around the big races whenever he could. Do you want me to call BJ Trucking?"

Joseph, bless his heart, was already on the phone to the company. Yes, they were based in Salt Lake City. Thank you, Google.

Joseph did a great job with the company. I resisted the urge to grab the phone away from him, but he was doing just fine. *Learn to delegate,Lieutenant.* He talked with human resources. Found out Colton was employed up until last week. Quit. Turned in his rig at Salt Lake. Has a PO box in Salt Lake. Joseph is still talking with the company and hands me the PO box info. I immediately go and call my postal inspector contact, good old Steve. He'll get back to me. Joseph has finished with the trucking company. No forwarding address.

"Hey, Lieutenant," says Joseph with a big smile. "I think we all ought to go to Salt Lake and talk to whoever we can at the company."

"We *all* can't go. Too much here to work."

Almost in unison Gary and Joseph say, "I'll go."

"Nice try guys. I'll go."

And I do. The weather is always questionable, but this has been a mild winter, I'm told. Can't prove it by me. Anyway, it is just over a three-hour drive.

Three hours, that's less than to Reno. Damn, I want to go to Reno.

I decide to stop in at the West Wendover P.D. It is the only other town in the county besides Elko with its own police department. We handle everything else. No wonder we are stretched so thin. West Wendover is on the eastern Nevada border with Utah. They have several casinos. Seems some Utahans enjoy the forbidden sport of gambling. West Wendover is a rapidly growing city.

Plenty of shopping and new housing for all the employees of the casinos and related businesses.

I meet with the chief. He's a solid cop. I immediately like him. He knows about our case and the flyers. He has had his officers checking trucks since the first ones came out over three years ago.

"When I heard you joined Elko's Sheriff's Office, I thought you might be the same officer from Santa Clara County who put out the original flyers. Then this last one comes out. Can I help in any way?"

I fill him in. We both offer to assist each other's department in any way we can. That's sort of understood, but when you make a face-to-face connection with someone it's always better.

I continue east into Utah on I-80, past the Great Salt Lake. Kind of yucky to look at. Not pretty. Before I make it to the trucking company, Steve calls me about the PO box. Already closed with no forwarding. Figures.

The trucking company officials are very cooperative. They let me talk with their dispatchers, but so much is being done with computers, G.P.S. and the internet, no one really knows the drivers personally anymore. Weaton/Colton has been working for BJ Trucking the whole time since he became Colton. His quitting was out of the blue. He gave no notice or reason why. Only comment on his separation papers was: "Time to move on."

So true, William Randall Weaton. But rest assured, I am coming for you.

Chapter 26

On the drive back to Elko I try to sort this all out. Weaton took over Colton's identity because he needed a valid commercial drivers' license. He had lost an eye and would be unable to meet the visual requirements for the CDL. Presuming Colton had a clean driving record, he would be eligible to be hired by any trucking company. So Weaton goes to work for BJ Trucking Lines as Colton. With a similar physical appearance no one would suspect he was anyone but the real Colton. The photo on the driver's license is all anyone would have to compare. We all know how "great" they are. Since the big trucking companies have little personal contact with their drivers, once he was hired, it worked.

Now Colton's CDL is getting close to expiring. It cannot be renewed except by a medical and vision exam. Weaton feels the need to take on a new identity and "Colton" will disappear. I keep wondering...where is Colton's body?

Weaton should feel an imminent threat from my flyers. They have influenced him to change his physical appearance a couple of times. The last incident, the woman from Wells, may have spooked him. I put out the flyer with the new changes to his appearance immediately after the murder.

My real concern now, not only has he made Colton disappear and taken on his identity, but he will need to replace him if he is going to continue driving a big rig. I want to apprehend him in the worst way. I do not want to be responsible for another trucker's death.

I get home and make my nightly call to Reno and the woman I want to see. Hearing her voice and our seemingly endless talks are wonderful, but I want to see her, hold her...well, you know.

She's in a feisty mood. "So are you ever coming here, or do I have to go to Elko in order to see you?"

Sounds like she's as anxious as I. "Actually, I'm pretty sure I can come this weekend, if you're free."

"Get your butt up here," she says in a sultry voice.

"I'm coming, woman; I'll be there."

We continue our usual nightly chatting. Eventually we say a lingering good-bye and hang up. God, I like that lady.

The next day the guys are already in the office when I arrive. Both look at me sheepishly. "What's up? You two did the town last night, right?"

"Only a couple of beers, Boss, you know me." Joseph admits. Gary, on the other hand, says nothing but nods. He drinks, I know he does, which is fine, I do. But he looks bright-eyed, not hung over. I'm glad they're connecting. We are becoming a team.

I get approval to be on leave the coming Friday and Monday. The week is now dragging by. I have the "boys" set up to keep busy while I'm gone. Gary's ready to be a full-time investigator. He's taking over cases and making good choices on his follow-ups. He is not wasting time, so far so good. Joseph is doing his usual excellent job.

Chapter 27

Friday morning, I leave for Reno driving "the Beast." This is on my dime, not the county's. Fine with me. The Porsche needs to get a run in; I miss driving him. The weather's good, no threats of nasty white stuff.

P.K. told me to come by her office, as she has a patient to see in the afternoon. When I get into town I check into my hotel and call her. I don't want to interrupt her while she is with a patient. She says, "Come over. Now."

"Yes, ma'am. I'm on my way."

I pull up to the building and start to walk toward her office when the door flies open. P.K. comes running out, throws her arms toward me, and draws me in for a hug. I tighten our embrace. We kiss. A long kiss. Then a few more. We stop to breathe and look at each other. We both start talking at the same time.

"God, it's so good to hold you."

"I couldn't wait for you to come."

We laugh. We laugh a lot. That's part of what makes our short relationship so amazing. We enjoy each other's company, even if it's only by phone.

P.K. looks lovely. She is wearing a gray jacket, white blouse, and black pants. So professional. She takes me inside.

"Make yourself at home; I just have to clean up

after my last appointment."

"Didn't happen to be a trucker, did it?"

She narrows her eyes at me. "I'm not sure if I'll get used to your dark humor."

Ooooh. Better back it down.

Then P.K. laughs and gives me her captivating smile. "Actually, I kind of enjoy it. What does that say about me?"

"Time for you to start hanging out with a cop?"

"I guess."

I look around the room. This is where she sees her patients. As expected, it is sterile and antiseptic looking, with a comfortable but specialized chair for the patient and many cabinets lining the walls. I also observe equipment I have never seen before and have no idea what its use is. I open a drawer. I jump back. It's full of eyeballs. They are in trays, but all are jiggling around. I close the drawer.

She catches me and laughs. "Some of my stock."

"I have never met anyone with a drawer full of eyeballs before."

"Good, one for me."

P.K. finishes her work and I decide to stop being snoopy. I'm not sure what I might find next.

P.K. is amused. "Big tough policeman can't handle some eyeballs, huh?"

"Just startled me. I'm okay with them."

"Don't feel bad, most men can't deal with them." She has finished her work, and it is time to go to dinner. "Do you like Mexican food?"

"Yeah, I love it. You mean we don't have to be chaperoned by big brother?"

"No. But you have to admit it's a pretty good idea

for a first date."

"You couldn't be safer than at your big brother's restaurant."

We decide I'll follow her from the office to her house and then we will go to the restaurant.

"Is that your Porsche?" She even pronounces it correctly, porsch-ah, as she heads straight for it. "I love them."

"Yes, it is. This is the Beast. That's his name."

"You name your cars. That's neat; I do, too. My Jeep is 'Baby.'" She points to a red Jeep Cherokee parked nearby. "It's great in the snow. How's the Porsche?"

"As long as the county gives me a 4-wheel drive I keep him out of it, but I have chains. Haven't used them yet. The plan is not to."

Her home is in a nice part of Reno, away from downtown. Newer house, good neighborhood, impressive.

Inside you can tell an artist lives here. Paintings and other pieces of art are on display, the home is tastefully decorated. She shows me some Native American paintings she is proud of. "I like Indian art."

"You need to meet Joseph. He has one above his desk, it's stunning. A family member did it."

"I plan on meeting your guys. I want to go to Elko and see what you're really up to." She gives me a sly look.

P.K. points to more artwork. They are mainly of women, especially their faces. I guess the proper word is...portraits. They're signed, *Kelly*. One is a Native American lady, with amazing eyes, the kind that follow you. Not creepy, but intense. I think she is trying to peer into my soul and see if I'm worthy. She's beautiful.

"Lady, you are a talent."

She smiles modestly. "Thank you. Let's go eat."

She directs me to an excellent Mexican restaurant. We have a long lingering dinner. Good margaritas, great food, and wonderful conversation. She asks if I have ever been to Lake Tahoe. Years ago, but since I don't gamble or ski, there wasn't much for me, except the beauty of the place.

"Want to take a drive up tomorrow? We can sightsee and eat and enjoy being together."

I place my hand on hers and entwine our fingers. Staring at her incredible face I tell her we should do just that. I take her home. At the door she slips into my embrace like she has always been there, so soft, and warm. I put my mouth on hers and the sensation is incredible. Nothing I have ever felt before; the kiss is long and lingering.

She gently breaks away from me. "Pick me up at ten and we can have breakfast and start our day."

"Ten it is."

She looks at me. "Better go," she says pressing her hand against my chest.

Damn. I do not want to leave. This is only our second official date, but we know each other's soul inside and out. But again, I think we both feel this is something too special to rush.

The next day, Saturday, we head to Tahoe and have an extraordinary time. We do exactly what she said: sightsee, eat, and relish each other's presence. We browse through the tourist shops and buy things for each other. She gets me a Tahoe T-shirt. I buy her some rocks she likes. Yes, the lady likes rocks, pretty ones, of course. Keeps them in her kitchen window in the sunlight.

We wind up on the south shore of the lake about dinner time. "Have you ever been on the paddle boats that tour the lake?" she asks.

"No, I haven't."

We park and go up to the box office. It's "all aboard" for the dinner cruise. This is fun. The Paddle boat begins to cruise across the lake and goes through Emerald Bay. It is appropriately named as the water is a gorgeous luminous green. As soon as it starts getting dark, they announce dinner. The meal is delicious and then the sound of a band begins. Time for dancing on the deck, under the stars. Oh hell. I don't dance. But I hold P.K. tight and try to act like I know what I'm doing. I do not think she's fooled. We are snuggled close together, so it doesn't matter. The hour is late when we finally dock and time to head "down the mountain" back to Reno.

It was a marvelous day. We held hands, kissed a few times, laughed, the time flew by. The main thing was we did not get tired or bored with each other. Being together is one big adventure. Boy, I like being with this lady. To be honest, it is becoming more than a *like* thing. I hope it is for her, too.

When we arrive at her house and reach the door, she opens it, steps in, and turns to look me in the eyes. "Want to come in?"

Always the graceful one, I trip trying to get inside before she changes her mind.

"That was elegant. Don't you cops have to pass a physical agility test?" Her humor is getting too close to mine.

She throws her arms around me and holds me close. "Want a glass of wine?"

Needless to say, the hotel room doesn't get used that night or the next. We spend a wonderful Sunday just wrapped around each other. She makes me breakfast. Hey, the artist can cook, too. We sit out on her patio for a while in the afternoon, while it is still somewhat warm, and read the Sunday paper. I could get used to this.

She "forages" in her kitchen, as she likes to say, and finds fixings for dinner. She prepares marinara sauce; it smells wondrous. She cooks up some pasta and we have a delectable dinner for two. There is French bread and red wine. Hmm, I wonder if there was some preplanning. I can only hope so.

Sunday goes by too fast. I need to go back to Elko tomorrow, and she has patients to see. We spend an exceptionally romantic evening and night together.

Monday morning P.K. starts to make breakfast.

I jump in, "What can I do?"

"Make toast and set the table."

I can handle that.

After breakfast I have to leave. We share a long goodbye. I get on the road and she goes to her office. Like a married couple. *Whoa, what did I say?*

You know, it just feels right.

Chapter 28

Back at the office I find the "boys" have not let me down. Gary has made an arrest on a case he originally handled when he was on patrol. Joseph went with him. Then they made two arrests on one of Joseph's cases.

"I should take more long weekends. Good work, guys."

"Please don't," Joseph whines. "Everyone keeps asking for you and we don't know how to answer their questions."

"Get used to it. I will definitely be gone more often."

Gary says, "How about we chip in and buy your lady a ticket to Elko, so you can stay close?"

"You know, I'm starting to like Reno more and more."

They groan.

"Okay, back to work. It'll be a while before anything happens either way. We're just getting to know each other."

"What's her real name?" Joseph asks. "Can't be P.K."

"Actually, it's Priscilla Killarney. It was bestowed on her by an Irish grandparent while her mother was too weak after childbirth to protest. She wasn't going be called 'Prissy' or 'Killie' Kelly so 'P. K.' she became."

"Don't blame her. My grandfather wanted to call

me 'he who wets pants.' Not funny," Joseph adds.

Nothing new has happened on the Weaton/Colton front. I expect another missing and presumed dead trucker. Of course, he may decide he can change jobs and maybe even use his old ID. You can live in this world with only one eye and even drive a vehicle, just not a commercial one. I have the dispatchers checking on all the above possibilities.

My personal cell phone rings. It's P.K. She never calls during the day.

"Hi, beautiful. Is everything okay?" I ask.

"No, I'm very much missing you. But that is not why I called. You remember I told you about my ocularist friend in Texas, who made the prosthetic eye for the trucker, Wheaties or whatever his name is? After you told me about the trucker, I called her. Got her voice mail and left a message."

"Yeah, and it's Weaton, but go on, my love."

"Whatever, she just called me. She had been on a long vacation. Guess what? She made him a replacement, only two days ago. Had so many voice mails, she just got to mine. She was trembling after I told her what he had done."

"What name did he use?"

"She said it was his old one, that's how she knew it was him. The Wheat one. You are such a stickler for details. I guess that's why you're good at what you do." She lowered her voice. "I know you're good at what you do; when are you coming back?"

"Oh, God woman, this business and pleasure mixing is tough."

"It would be easier if you were here," she purrs.

"Or if you were here."

"I've been weighing that. We both have a lot going for us where we're at now."

"I know. No decision must be made yet; I can travel. The road is getting shorter each trip."

"I can drive, too, you know. 'Baby' takes good care of me. Just wait for the better weather. I still want to check out your world."

"Fair enough. And to get back to my world, did your friend say if he left an address?"

"Yes, Officer, I knew you would ask, and no, he did not. He made the appointment a week before. Showed up on time and paid cash. No real small talk except he mentioned he wanted to be in Florida for the Daytona 500. How's that, Investigator? I can be a good partner, huh?"

"I love you. You're the best."

"Don't ever forget it. No one will ever love you more than I do."

How am I supposed to go back to work?

All right, this means he will be in Florida in February. I may not fish or hunt, but I know my racing. Wonder if P.K. would like to go to the Daytona 500? A thought. It isn't even Thanksgiving yet, so I try to think of his next move. My mind is whirling with ideas, none of them solid enough to move on.

Joseph and Gary continue to do great work. I do my paperwork stuff and help with cases. We're a good team. This allows me more time to check on any angle I can think of with Weaton/Colton and look for any sign of another missing trucker or body.

I go to Reno as much as possible, and even have Thanksgiving dinner with P.K. and her brother's family. The "big guy" is a sweet lovable Irishman. I feel warm and comfortable with the clan. I am informed I will be in Reno for Christmas...no argument from me.

As I walk into the office my phone is ringing. It's the dispatch supervisor.

"We found Colton." She sounds excited.

Colton has been found—or at least a body matching his description with his CDL and identification. This information is from the Arizona Highway Patrol. By the time I get to her office she has highway patrol on the phone.

She hands me the phone and I speak to the captain overseeing the case. Apparently, a trucker had stopped alongside Interstate 40 between Kingman and Flagstaff. He needed to pee. (How many crimes are discovered by drivers needing to relieve themselves?) It is a mountainous area. As he was doing his business, he looked over the side of the cliff. It was just after sunrise; the sun was shining clear and bright. Looking farther down he saw a body hanging over a culvert, which was protruding from the cliff. The patrol captain thinks whoever tossed the body off the cliff did so at night and was not aware of the culvert. A few feet in any other direction and the body would have gone down a couple of hundred more feet and probably never been noticed. The body was a white male in his forties, blond hair, and blue eyes. Colton had some papers from JB Trucking in his pockets. His face was severely smashed. Possibly from the fall, but the captain didn't think the distance was enough for the amount of damage to the face.

"Does he have two eyes?"

The captain tells me, "Yes, he does."

He was notified when the name of the victim came

up on a "hit" with the computer system. He remembered my flyers. "I was just calling you when your office got through first. He matches your description of the original Colton, except he is probably only five-foot-nine at best. He is also heavier than your 175 pounds but close enough. He killed again, didn't he? This is your Weaton fellow?"

"Yes. I've been expecting this."

"So we do not really have Colton, do we? We have to ID this poor guy as soon as possible."

"Absolutely; any help we can offer, just call. This is Weaton's new identity, and I bet this guy is a trucker."

"Sounds like a good bet. I am having the body sent to the state's coroner in Phoenix. They have a good forensics lab. I'll keep you updated. The fingerprints will probably be the solution; they seem to be untouched."

The fingerprints. Yes, Weaton probably figured the body would never be found, so no worry. The real Colton is somewhere similar, only his body has not been located yet.

For some time now, I've been taking coffee breaks at the local truck stops. I talk with drivers and try to learn their way of life, searching for anything that might help. The drivers are more than willing to talk to me. They are becoming increasingly aware they may be a target. I've been told there have been occasional scuffles in truck stops across the country when one driver tries to approach another. The word's out and they are on edge. I've even been contacted by a trucker's "blog," an internet website for long-haul truckers. It keeps them updated on their crazy world.

The sheriff gave me approval to talk with these folks.

"Anything to catch the murdering S.O.B.," were his exact words.

Chapter 29

Two days later, the Arizona captain calls me. "We have a match with the fingerprints from the body. He is Earnest William Bennett. Forty-six years old. You're right, he was a trucker. His CDL was issued out of Huntsville, Alabama. Has four years left until expiration. I have already asked the police department there for help. I'll let you know when I hear anything. I'm thinking your boy partnered up with Bennett somewhere, murdered him, and is in Bennett's truck headed west. What's your thoughts?"

"Exactly the same. If Weaton follows his usual M.O., you will find Bennett has little or no contact with any family. That's how Colton was."

"How'd you get onto Colton as being the new Weaton?"

"Colton missed his mother's birthday. They never heard from him otherwise, only on Mom's birthday. His family became worried. They contacted the police. He was a real loner."

We hang up promising to keep each other informed of any new facts.

I ponder this information for a while. Then I go the dispatch supervisor. She has gotten into the case and is motivated. I ask her to search for Bennett in any public records anywhere she can. Especially traffic tickets. I tell her not to give up on Weaton or Colton. We don't know what this crazy killer has been up to or how he's thinking now.

Credit checks, yes, any banking or cards, anything would help.

I call FBI Andy. He can get bank records and other financial stuff we mere commoners cannot. He takes my information and will start checking. Good to talk with Andy again, been too long. He's been able to avoid the eastern part of Nevada and is happily working in the Lake Tahoe office.

Lake Tahoe. I think of P.K. again. What a great time we had there. The day cemented our relationship. I can still see us standing on the deck of the paddleboat going across the lake in the darkness. My arms around her. Moonlight splashing over the water. Next to the moon was a swirl of a windswept clouds. It was as if the hand of God was signing his piece of art.

Back to the present. I am driving myself crazy with all the what-ifs, how-abouts, and maybes. I need to get working on local cases. The Arizona Highway Patrol, FBI, and dispatchers will keep busy on the checks for now.

I go out to the guys and growl, "Give me something to do or I'll just take off for Reno. This case is driving me bananas."

They both grab papers from their desks and run up to me. "Don't go, Boss; it'll be fine. Here. We can keep you so busy you won't think of it or her," Joseph pleads.

Gary says, "He won't stop thinking of her, that's obvious, but a couple of files will at least help."

I love these guys, we're a becoming a family.

I take some cases from them and go back to my

office. About thirty minutes later an armed robbery in progress call is broadcast on the Elko PD radio. We monitor them as well as our own.

Action!

I'm on my feet and the guys are at the door. Like children, *can we go, Dad, please?* Hell, yes, we can go. We all dash to the parking lot and race off in our individual units. This is what it's all about. The adrenaline rush. Investigations is good, but nothing beats the thrill of the chase, the chance for action. Let's face it, none of us got into this silly job to sit in an office and pore through files looking for clues. Investigations is a good spot to gravitate to, but street work is in our souls.

The robbery occurred at a casino/hotel near I-80. A casino security officer exchanged gunfire with one of the suspects. According to the radio, security got a license plate and description of the getaway car. Two persons were in the vehicle. This is big city stuff; does not usually happen here. The suspect vehicle was last seen heading onto I-80 westbound. I radio both guys to head toward the on ramp to the west, hoping we can get ahead of the suspect.

I'm in the lead. Tires squeal as we turn onto the freeway. Lights and sirens on, we are an impressive procession. Gary and I in our SUVs and Joseph in his pickup truck. All unmarked except for the lights in the grills.

Our luck holds and the suspect vehicle is right in front of us. Our timing is perfect. We're on him. Gary and I close on the car. Joseph is behind us. Suddenly the suspect slams on his brakes and swings into the median. Gary and I make evasive moves and we both dive our vehicles into the median after him. The suspect vehicle almost flips with the severity of his turn but keeps upright and stays in the median heading toward the east bound lanes of the freeway. Good old Joseph heads straight toward the suspect. He is not letting up. The suspect must think "That crazy cop is going to kill me." The suspect turns sharply and spins out in the soft, muddy median. He tries to keep moving but he is mired in the mud. We jam on our brakes and jump out, our weapons pointed at the suspects.

"Hands! Show your hands!"

Wisely, they do as ordered. We get them out of the vehicle and handcuff them. The vehicle is checked. The money is in a paper bag in the back seat and a .38 revolver is on the floor. Two rounds had been fired.

Then Elko PD comes racing up. Three patrol cars and a sergeant. The sergeant jumps out and runs up next to us. I hear more coming. "Must be shift change, Sarge; I didn't know you had this many units. I believe you want to talk with these gentlemen?"

"Thank you, Lieutenant. The City of Elko is grateful for the county's assistance. We'll take it from here." He grins sarcastically.

My guys and I high-five and whoop and holler. "It's close to quitting time and we're much too pumped up to sit at a desk. I say it is pizza and beer time. My treat."

The vote is unanimous. We place ourselves off duty and go to the pizza parlor. Good bonding time. We replay the "great chase" over and over.

"Joseph, you were on it. I thought you were going to hit him. Good move."

"I was trying to hit him. I hate that truck."

"You said you wanted a pickup instead of a SUV."

"I didn't want a baby blue one. It's humiliating."

We stay a couple of hours and have a couple of beers. Then we all head our separate ways. I'm going to have a good story to tell P.K. for our nightly chat.

Chapter 30

P.K. is not impressed with my story of our heroics. "You could have been killed or injured. I thought you were supposed to interview people and solve crimes, not go off chasing armed robbers through the streets."

"Honey, a crime was committed. We were able to apprehend the perpetrators. It's our duty."

"Bull. You guys just wanted to get out of the office and in on the action. Boys playing cops and robbers. Please be careful, Baby. I love you and want us together."

That went well. We continue talking for some time as usual. She calms down but makes me promise to be extra careful. Christmas is coming very soon, and I'll be going to Reno. We discuss presents for each other. She's very coy about what I can get her. But in all fairness so am I. We are getting to know each other's heart and soul but not so much worldly things. Actually, that says a lot for our relationship. Jewelry would be a good idea. I am nothing if not observant. This lady likes her bling. The good stuff, not costume jewelry.

The following morning, Undersheriff George comes into my office. He closes the door. He has a somber look. "I was in my office yesterday when the armed robbery call came in. The next thing I saw out my window was you guys running to your vehicles and roaring out of the parking lot. I closed my eyes and looked to the heavens. 'Lord, please don't let them do anything stupid.' And you didn't. I listened to you commanding your troops. I was following your pursuit then all went silent. When I heard you radio, 'suspects in custody,' I could breathe again. You made us proud. Any time we can look good in front of another agency is the best. Nice job you and your men did yesterday."

Well, that went better than my phone call last night. I probably won't tell P.K. about George's prayer. She would not see the humor in it.

George stops to congratulate the guys. *Nice touch, George.* I appreciate it. Just before he walks out the door the Elko radio goes off again. This time it's a bank robbery in downtown Elko. *What the hell is this?* This is not typical Elko. Oh yeah, it is Christmas time. Doesn't matter where you are, crime goes up during the holidays. All three of us head toward the door. George looks at the ceiling and puts his hands together. Didn't know George was such a religious man. Then he smiles, sort of. Off we go.

This time the suspect is on foot; a citizen is following the perp and calling 911 from his cell phone. The guy goes into a parking lot and the good Samaritan loses sight of him. The PD units are in the area, then a black SUV speeds out of the lot. The guys and I are on a street between the highway and the SUV. I tell them to turn off the emergency lights, so he won't see us. Sure enough, here comes the black SUV a couple of blocks away.

"Wait, wait, now hit the lights and let's block the street."

Gary and I slide in front of the SUV but it tries to

make a move to the other side of the street. Out of nowhere comes Joseph's truck. He drills the SUV. Game over. The driver is too stunned to flee. Elko comes up and takes over. The sergeant looks at me and shakes his head.

"Maybe we should just shut down Elko PD while you three are on duty. Apparently, we're not needed."

"Sarge, somebody has to do the booking and the reports."

He laughs and shakes all our hands. This has been fun, but we seriously have our own work to do.

"Too early for beer and pizza, guys; back to the office. Ah, Joseph, I think you have an accident report to file."

He grins.

When we walk in the door of our building several of the department employees are waiting. They give us a big cheer. George is standing behind them. Huge grin. He gives us a "thumbs up." *Whew.* I'll mention Joseph's truck later.

No more fun and games… We dig into our cases. Joseph and Gary go out to conduct follow-ups and I settle into trying to find a commonality to some recent home burglaries. Again, typically crime increases during the holiday season. The victims all live in upper scale areas. Residents are not home when the houses are hit. The initial reports from patrol officers are good. No fingerprints are found except those of the family members. Gloves must have been used. Entry is from the rear of the residence, usually breaking a door or window. Jewelry, money, and other small valuable items are taken. We have a long list of stolen items. Some of the victims were smart enough to have made photo inventories of their valuables. The reports show no connection between the victims. This M.O. has a pattern. Probably the same perpetrators.

I start to contact the victims. One by one I ask all sorts of questions to try to determine a connection. I find a commonality. All are business owners. All belong to the Elko Chamber of Commerce. I drop in on Davis, the Elko city detective who handles the burglaries occurring within the city limits. I have the ones from the unincorporated county area. He confirms he has had a rash of similar burgs. We compare notes. All upscale homes and all business owners. All with Chamber membership. We call the Chamber office and ask if they've had a meeting lately. Yes, they have. The first of December. A mixer where a new member was introduced. A burglar alarm company. It went very well, we're told. The new member offered each member a free security analysis of their homes.

A quick follow-up with the victims tells us they all had taken the "new member" up on his offer. A couple of them had even wanted to sign up for the alarm system. Guess what. They had not heard back yet from the salesman. We get his number from them and dial it: *"The number you are calling is no longer in service or has been disconnected."*

Now Davis and I must find Larry Thomson. Probably not this real name. We have our respective patrol officers checking any hotels or motels for guests who checked in around the first of December and checked out a week or so ago around the time of the last burglary. We put out an alert to other law enforcement agencies to make them aware of the scam. Twin Falls,

Idaho reports they, too, were hit by the "Larry Thompson" scam, right before Thanksgiving. A heads-up would have been nice, Twin Falls.

We call him the Holiday Bandit.

One of the Elko Patrol units has some info from a motel. A man and woman had been staying there since the end of November—until six days ago. The name given was Edward Peterson. A credit card was used at checkout. A vehicle description on the guest card was for a Cadillac with Colorado plates. Davis and I head over to the motel. The gentleman was a "sales type," according to the clerk. He checked the license plate and found the customer had inverted the license numbers on his registration. I ask if he always checked the plate numbers. He said it was company policy. They have a problem with guests leaving unpaid bills. *Great policy.* Now an APB (All Points Bulletin) is broadcast for the Cadillac along with Peterson's identification information.

I call FBI Andy to see if he can check on Peterson's credit card for recent activity. Of course, he can; the FBI can do anything.

One of the victims calls me. She received a phone call from a pawn shop in South Lake Tahoe. Ah...Lake Tahoe; do not get me started. Anyway, the pawn shop took in some jewelry and when the owner was checking the items, he noticed what appeared to be a phone number engraved on the back of a Patek Philippe ladies' watch. I play dumb because *ladies' watch* was all I got. I find out it is an awfully expensive line of timepieces. The pawn shop owner called the number and got the victim. She told him it was stolen and had been reported to the police. He gave her his number and told her about the other items he had. None were hers or her husband's. The victim tells me she bought the watch on a trip to Switzerland. I can't remember what business she and her husband had but it sounds like a good one to me.

I immediately call FBI Andy again. Since South Lake Tahoe is in California, that makes this interstate transportation of stolen goods. The good old FBI can get in on this kind of stuff. Andy's already on it. He found out Peterson's credit card was used at Caesars Hotel Casino, located on the Nevada side of the state line. He used it to book a room three days ago. Apparently, he is still a guest. Andy will go to the pawn shop and see what else they have. He will also check on the other area pawn shops. Being across the state line from the casinos, the California side has plenty of pawn shops. They are happy to assist the losers with money to get back home or to go gamble some more.

FBI Andy says, "Why don't you come up and we can do this together? You were planning on going to Reno to see your lady for Christmas, right? We can get this wrapped up and both get to Christmas on time. And you can do it on the county's time and vehicle."

Whoever said the FBI wasn't clever? "Great idea, Andy. I'm going to my boss right now and I'll let you know."

George also thinks it's a good idea to be involved so "we" can get the local press for solving the case and apprehending the bad guys. Christmas is only a few days away, so I will be able to start my vacation on schedule and use the county vehicle for the trip. The caveat is we catch Peterson before he moves on. Since he has moved just prior to each holiday, I think he is

171

planning to stay in Tahoe for Christmas.

I tell the guys what's going on. They resign themselves to the fact they will have to function without me for a week or two.

"Can I help you pack?"

"I'll get your vehicle gassed up."

Yeah, they'll be fine.

Chapter 31

I call P.K. and tell her about the trip to Tahoe.

"You don't have to stay in Tahoe, do you? You can stay with me, can't you?"

"Try and keep me away."

"When will you be here?"

"About one or one-thirty."

"Tomorrow afternoon?"

"No, tonight. I'm leaving right now."

"Now? It's dark now; you be careful."

"My love, I have headlights."

"Smart aleck, please be careful."

"I will. I promise."

She lowers her voice to the sultry tone she has. "I'll leave the lights on for you."

I make the trip in record time. The NHP has apparently taken the night off since l encounter none.

As I pull up to P.K.'s house I note *all* the lights are on. I see her peeking out the window. She's out the door and into my arms. God, this woman feels good to hold. She helps me get my stuff out of the car and into the house we go. We don't get a lot of sleep, but it's a good night. I must get up early to meet with Andy in Tahoe, and P.K. must get to work for a client first thing in the morning. We may be sleepy but we're happy. I love this woman; it feels right with her.

I drive "up the hill" as the locals say about the

drive to Tahoe. I meet Andy at his office in South Lake. He's wearing a down vest and a flannel shirt. What is this?

"You're still with the Bureau, aren't you?" I ask. He ignores my comment.

Andy's checked with the local pawn shops and has identified several items from the Elko burglaries. His partner is already at Caesars monitoring the suspect.

Andy was able to locate him last night with help from the casino security and watched him gambling big time at the 21 tables. A lady was with him. Andy thinks she was wearing some of the stolen jewelry.

We first go to the pawn shop that called my victim. The owner shows me the watch. I have a photo of the watch from the victim's jewelry inventory. It matches. The employee who took in the watch recognizes Peterson's picture from the driver's license photo Andy received from the Colorado DMV. That's enough for us. The details on the other items can wait. We need to arrest this guy before he changes his plans.

We go to Caesars and meet with Andy's partner. He doesn't look like an FBI agent either. Looks more like a ski bum: sweater, Levis, boots. Take them out of the big cities and they almost look normal. It is about eleven a.m. and the suspects are still in their room.

The casino security supervisor accompanies us with a pass key. Room service dishes are outside the door. Had breakfast; good, they should be up. Andy's partner knocks on the door. We all know the familiar... knock, knock, knock... "housekeeping, housekeeping." He uses a falsetto voice. He's almost too good at this.

We're all on the sides of the door out of view of the peep hole. As the lock slides open Andy motions the security officer to stay back. Door opens and we burst inside, weapons drawn.

"FBI. You're under arrest." Andy's just got to be first. *Show off.* "Hands; show your hands."

The suspects are caught flatfooted. Classic entry on our part. The woman identified as Peterson's wife has on a necklace I recognize from the photo inventory my victim had given me. More stolen items are found in their luggage.

We hook them up and take them down to the Douglas County jail. Andy's partner heads to the parking lot and has the Cadillac towed to a storage yard. It too, has some items of interest. Some of it is from the Twin Falls caper and others are from who knows where. Busy couple.

With them cooling their heels waiting for an attorney, Andy and I go to lunch. His partner joins us after the car is secured.

Two days until Christmas and now I'm trying to come up with an appropriate gift for P.K. I have bought a few things, but I'm searching for the *outstanding* gift. No luck so far. The jewelers in Elko haven't been inspiring. Cowboy jewelry isn't P.K.'s thing, I know that much. Andy's no help as I think he has his wife believing a new vacuum cleaner is a wonder gift, but his partner is more help. He is single and has been for some time. He tells me of a local jeweler who has helped him out in the past. After lunch we head over there. Located in one of the big hotel/casinos, this place is high end. I feel my credits cards trying to escape from my wallet. They know they are about to be abused.

The owner knows Andy's partner. Apparently from

many transactions. I'm given the "This is my good old friend, what can you do for him?" introduction.

The jeweler is excellent. He asks me some questions about my relationship with P.K. and I tell him how much our trip to Tahoe meant. He nods, walks over to a case, and brings out some charms. Believe it or not he has a gold paddleboat charm like the one we rode on. We apparently were not the first couple to find it a romantic trip.

We look at other charms. I spy one that looks like an eye.

"That's an Egyptian all-seeing eye," he says. I take it also.

He has one of the Reno arch, a big tourist landmark, so I add it, too.

"Don't forget a bracelet," says Andy's partner.

Must be gold, of course, nothing but the best. I settle on an 18-carat one. Looks delicate but still sturdy enough for the three charms with room for more. I have no doubt we will have more great memories to add.

"Good job," Andy's partner says. "You'll be a hit."

I get the "friend of the FBI" discount, whatever that is, and walk out with the kind of special present I wanted. I'm pleased. This does have our memories on it.

Back at the office, Andy looks at us and smiles.

"While you two were Christmas shopping, I took care of this."

He has all the recovered jewelry already tagged and boxed for me. We go back to the pawn shops to check the rest of the pawned items. There is quite a haul. Most of it's from Elko, some from Twin Falls, and some we can't identify. We confiscate it all. Since the Petersons pawned them, they are probably on some other agencies' lists somewhere.

It's now the end of the day and I am almost officially on leave. Andy offers to keep the items in his office so it will have a proper "chain of evidence." Having the evidence sitting in my vehicle at P.K.'s house for a week will not cut it. I thank Andy and his partner, and head "down the hill." Good day, good job. I call George and bring him up to date. He's quite pleased.

"Enjoy your Christmas. You deserve it."

"Merry Christmas to you, too, George. See you next week."

I call P.K. who tells me we are invited to her brother's restaurant for his employees' Christmas party. I want to have my own party just with her, but it's a good feeling to be included as part of her family already. Besides, we have a long week ahead.

Chapter 32

The party at the restaurant is a blast. P.K.'s brother and his wife put on a good time for their employees. The place is closed to the public. The whole idea is the employees do not have to work. The family waits on them. This includes P.K. and me. I'm treated like family; I handle the bar. Not the first bar I *handled*. I have a ball. P.K. and a niece serve the food. Big guy and his wife do the cooking. Very classy. Apparently, some of the employees have been there for a long time. I can see why.

I tell P.K. she looks quite at ease being a waitress. She said she had to work at it once and hated it. But for the brother's party she enjoys it.

"Once a year it's fun. They have a good staff. They have one waitress I always threaten to spill food on because she did it to me once. I always feel completely at ease here."

The staff feels protective of P.K....more than one tells me what a nice lady she is, and I better be good to her. This also includes the waitress who spilled food on her.

Hell, the size of her brother is message enough for me.

We all help with clean-up. While we are all working and laughing her brother says to me, "You've been busy out there in Elko. I saw you made the papers with some of your arrests."

Being modest I say, "We were simply in the right place to help out."

"Right place; you boys risked life and limb to get to the right place. Yeah, and the next day you go and catch a bank robber. I didn't realize so much happened in Elko."

"Robert? What bank robber?" P.K.'s head comes up and her beautiful eyes narrow.

I'm dead.

"I haven't had a chance to tell you about the robbery. It was no big thing; Joseph caught him. We were just driving down the street…"

"Robert, that's what I call a lie by omission. You could have told me last night. You knew I'd be upset."

"Uh, we were busy...uh...tired last night. I was going to tell you tonight."

Brother and family chuckle and get back to the clean-up. They have seen the "wrath of P.K." before.

On the way to her house, she admonishes me again about not telling her. Then she snuggles up to me as I'm driving.

"Please, please be careful. I just found you; I don't want to lose you."

The night goes well. The next day she doesn't have to work so we hang out. We do this best. Just enjoy being a couple. P.K. has decorated the house for the holidays. Tree and everything. Very tasteful and festive.

She tells me she hasn't put up Christmas decorations for some time. This is the first year she has wanted to. To celebrate with me. My heart is touched. The next day is Christmas Eve. She likes to do the gifts on Christmas Eve. Great with me, we will be alone since Christmas morning we're going to the brother's home. We have a meat and cheese tray to nibble on while enjoying the evening. A little wine and we are ready to open presents.

I'm nervous. I want this to be special for her.

We open some smaller gifts for each other. Some are funny and some are thoughtful. I have properly found "her perfume." *Good job, Robert.* I peeked on the last visit. She got me some manly aftershave I've never heard of, but I like it. Okay, she likes it, so I like it. She bought me a couple of genuinely nice shirts. And then we get to the "big" presents. We have both kept back a present each.

"You first."

"No, you first."

I go first. I open a nicely wrapped small box. Inside is a gold bracelet. Very manly, sturdy enough for me, and yet beautiful. It looks expensive. I'm touched by her thoughtfulness.

"Like it?"

"Love it; I've never had anything this nice." I grab her and give her a long kiss. She describes the fine points of the bracelet. This gal knows her jewelry. I hope my gift is up to snuff. I give it to her.

She opens it like a lady. No tearing of paper, just carefully removing the wrapping. Then opens the box.

"Robert, where did you find this? I love it. The paddleboat, the eye, even the Reno arch. I love it. This is us. These are our memories." She squeals with joy.

The week flies by. Christmas day with the family. Really nice. I feel like part of the family more every day. I don't want to leave, and she doesn't want me to go.

New Year's Eve is spent at the restaurant, as guests this time. New Year's Day is a quiet snuggle day. The next morning, I must go to the lake, meet with Andy, and get my evidence. Then head back to Elko.

Extremely hard to leave her in the morning. We decide we belong together in the same place. We're just not sure where that place is going to be.

Chapter 33

When I walk into the office in Elko, Joseph and Gary are at their desks, appearing to be working diligently. *Knew I was coming.*

They fill me in on what has been going on. They have been busy, so they say.

"Have a good Christmas, Bob?"

"Absolutely the best. How about you two?"

"I had Gary over to Mom's for Christmas dinner."

"Did he behave himself?"

"Of course, I did. Never pass up a home-cooked meal. Great food."

"So, Joseph, what did the undersheriff say about your accident report?"

"Oh, I forgot to give it to him."

"*Joseph.* I told you to give it to him first thing the next day."

Joseph smiles. "Relax, boss, I gave it to him. He said, 'good job' but try not to total any vehicles in the future."

"Always the jokester, aren't you?"

"Yeah, but you're almost as good as I am."

"What have you been driving?"

"An old Chevy pickup from the parks department, I think. Or maybe sanitation. Someone's been carrying a lot of poop in it."

"What color is the truck?"

"White."

"Okay, so you won't be wrecking it until your replacement arrives. If you get one."

Joseph scowls.

Gary notices my bracelet. "Christmas present, I presume."

"Yes." I proudly show it off. Joseph puts a keen eye to it.

"She did well, Bob. Hope yours was up to this standard."

I assure him it was and describe the charms and bracelet.

"Ahhh, that's neat. You did right by her." Joseph smiles approvingly.

I log all my evidence in from Tahoe and get my report ready for the DA.

Next, I go see George. He is proud as punch.

"Great work. The sheriff's happy as hell. Election year, you know. We need to keep the press positive. He's a good boss, you realize?"

"So are you, George. You have been quite supportive of me and my unit. I appreciate it."

The brown-nosing done; I need to go back to work.

I check with the dispatch supervisor on Weaton, et al., for any news. Nothing. I check my messages. The Arizona captain handling the dead trucker has left me a couple of calls. I call him back. He has news from the Huntsville, Alabama police. As I suspected, Bennett, the dead trucker, was not close with family. However, they knew he had his own truck. He was an owner-operator and would hire on with various companies. Unfortunately, the family did not know who he was working for at present. The captain ran a nationwide check to find a truck registration for Bennett. The truck was registered in Alabama. After an APB was put out for Bennett's truck the captain was contacted by a California police department. The truck had been found abandoned in a truck stop in San Bernardino. The trailer was not with it. Apparently Weaton completed the delivery. That would alleviate any red flags. Then he abandoned Bennett's tractor. The captain had the California authorities do a full crime scene investigation on the tractor. Two DNA samples came up along with a lot of blood. Probably poor Bennett's. It appeared he was attacked in the bunk of the sleeper cab. Weaton probably waited until he fell asleep and bludgeoned him to death.

DNA is new to law enforcement and is the wave of the future for solving crimes. Once we identify Bennett's sample, then the other sample should be Weaton. I hope. Then we can compare blood samples from the other crimes he is suspected of committing. I already have some solid evidence against him, but a DNA match would nail him down on all the murders, especially *my case*.

The Arizona captain and I agree that keeping Bennett's truck was too dangerous for Weaton. He has the ID and now can go to work for a long-haul company and drive their trucks. Bennett's driving record is clean; he would be hired by any company. Especially as there is a growing shortage of licensed drivers nationwide.

We are back to square one. Chasing a shadow.

Chapter 34

I make several trips to Reno and the lady I love.

God, I do love that woman. The nightly phone calls are good but being together is heavenly. With the spring weather coming P.K. is planning on coming to Elko to "see my world." I can't wait. But I'm nervous about it. If she hates it, what will we do? I have already talked about getting a job closer to Reno. She will have none of that talk.

"You have a position there. No, you stay there. You're doing great and they seem to like you. So why not stay?"

"Because you're not here. I'm afraid you won't like Elko."

"You're there. That's all I need. You. End of discussion."

"Yes, ma'am."

A few days later the door to the office flies opens and in walks Charlie.

"Charlie, what the hell?"

"The wife and I are taking a motor home trip and I thought Elko was a good place to spend a few days."

Charlie and I have been talking on and off since I moved here. His wife always wanted to tour the country in a motor home. He was always against the idea. He didn't tell me they got one.

"Part of the deal was I get to come here and check

on you. Then we'll take the damned trip."

"Thank you, Charlie, but I'm fine."

"No, you're not. You haven't found Colton's body and you don't have Weaton yet. Besides, that Reno woman is driving you crazy. You need to marry her and settle down. And I do not mean anywhere else but here. I was talking with George and the sheriff. They're pretty happy with you. Don't get any crazy ideas about moving to Reno. You got a future here."

"Anything else, Dad?"

"Yes, I miss you, damn it." He stomps over and gives me a big bear hug.

I manage to choke out, "I miss you, too, Charlie."

Charlie, Charlie. I'm dumbstruck. I knew we got along well, but damn; I feel like he is my dad.

We agree to meet for dinner at a nice restaurant. He's already tired of eating in the motor home. I offer to pick him and his wife up. He says no, they are pulling a small car behind the motor home.

"Charlie, if memory serves me correctly, you hated seeing motor homes towing a car. Said it was redundant."

"That son of a bitch is so big I can hardly park it in a truck stop, let alone on a city street. If we didn't have the car, we'd probably starve to death or at least dehydrate from lack of alcoholic beverage."

It is wonderful to see Charlie's wife again, always pleasant, and uplifting. We have a great time. We tell jokes, mostly at Charlie's expense, of course the perpetual war stories, and get around to the case as I knew we would. Mrs. Charlie is used to this stuff. Only difference is she can't excuse herself to clean up tonight.

Finally, she tactfully suggests, "Why don't we go back to the RV Park and let these poor restaurant people go home?"

Good move: then she can excuse herself and let us talk shop all night as we used to. And we do. Charlie thinks Colton is one of the unidentified bodies that shows up now and then in a recycling plant. Some are dismembered, some are not. Some have been determined to have been dead for months or years. How they wind up in a recycling plant years later is unknown. Good theory, I tell him.

"But I check on every unidentified dead body that pops up," I assure him. "None is close enough in description to Colton to follow up."

"Okay, you're doing fine. We will be leaving in the morning. Just had to check." He smiles an un-Charlie-like warm smile. He doesn't smile often.

We say our good-byes and Mrs. Charlie comes out to gives me a big hug. "You marry that girl. She seems right for you, Bob."

I go home and call P.K. It's late but she told me to call whenever I got back. A sleepy voice answers. "Hi, honey. How was dinner?"

"Mom and Dad think I should marry you. I told them I agreed."

"I'm up for that. They should come to the wedding."

"Definitely."

We talk for a little while longer. P.K. says she's been thinking about my "Wheaties" man, as she calls him. Last time I was in Reno she asked for one of the flyers with his photos and my added artwork.

"Being an artist who loves faces, I had to touch up

your 'after' drawings of what you think he looks like now. I love you, darling, and you are incredibly talented in your own way, but an artist, you are not. Is there any way you could get his x-rays from when he was injured? That way I could get his facial structure correct."

"Well, well, seems like I may be getting more than a partner for life; I may also be getting a partner in crime fighting. You little devil, you never cease to amaze me with your talents. I'll see what I can do about it."

The next morning, I call Gregg, the Enid, Oklahoma detective. I tell him what we're trying to do. Of course, we all know medical records are protected by the Patient Privacy Act, but since we have homicide warrants out for Weaton, he will see what he can do. He is still seeing Gloria, Weaton's ex, so that may facilitate the matter.

The next morning Gregg calls me. He has a copy of the x-rays. He'll mail them to me. I don't ask how he got them, and he doesn't say.

Chapter 35

Now that Charlie has brought it up again, I *would* like to find Colton's body. I don't need it for a conviction with all the other bodies and evidence involved, but it is a loose end.

I get the x-rays from Greg and give them to P.K. on my next visit. She has made several drawings of his face already. Definitely better than my work.

She takes the x-rays and studies them intently. "I need to change the cheek bones more and he also has jaw damage. He lost some teeth in the accident. He had more than a new eye replaced. He had to have a partial made to replace the missing teeth."

P.K. makes new drawings of Weaton with his various "disguises." Hair, no hair, dark hair, blond hair, mustache, beard, sunglasses, regular glasses, hat, and no hat.

While she's working, I can tell she is at her happiest. She loves being creative. Mesmerizing watching her. These are not just "wanted poster" drawings, they're pieces of art.

A sexy forensic artist. And she is mine.

Some weeks later as I'm getting ready for work, I get this odd feeling. I have always been one who gets feelings. Usually, I'm right. Whatever it is, it has served me well in police work.

Joseph and I have talked about these things. He

finds it normal. His grandfather is a shaman, after all.

He tells me to always, "Go with your gut, boss. Gary, on the other hand, listens to another part of his body."

When Joseph and I are having these discussions, Gary puts his head down and goes back to work.

Anyway, this morning I get the urge to turn on the TV morning news. I never do that.

The bright-eyed newsperson is just starting a breaking news story: "A man missing for years has turned up in a Las Vegas psychiatric ward."

I keep watching. The man's name is *David Colton*. The story goes on to say he was a meth user and has been living on the streets of Las Vegas. He was struck by a car and was hospitalized for his injuries. Because of his addiction he was placed in a drug rehab facility, then his behavior become so bizarre he was placed in the psychiatric facility. Now, apparently because he's off drugs, he's lucid and talking with the staff. The facility contacted the Las Vegas Metro Police Department who was able to identify Colton as being reported missing by his family several years ago.

My brain tilted. *Colton alive?* It could be him. Homeless on the street, a meth head, he didn't need to be dead.

When I walk into the office the guys look white as ghosts. Even Joseph.

"Bob, come here; we just got this email from Las Vegas Metro. They have Colton."

"I know. I saw it on the news."

"Man, you're always ahead of us. Can't surprise you with anything."

The email has replaced the old teletype we used to

get from other agencies. Metro saw my APBs in the system and contacted us. There's a place for computers, I guess. It's difficult for me to realize how much police work has changed in the few years, *I think* since I started.

I get on the phone with the Metro detective handling the case. He says they have confirmed the fingerprints and the man is David Allen Colton. He tells them he was a truck driver. He also tells the officer he was given meth by another driver and somehow became an addict, living on the streets of Vegas.

Colton is still in the psych facility. I tell the detective I'll be coming down to interview him. I also tell him Colton needs to be in protective custody. His life may be in danger. Now that his story is in the news, Weaton may see it and not want him remembering anything. The detective asks about notifying the family, as there's a missing person report in the system. I ask him to wait until I can talk with Colton.

I discuss with George about getting to Las Vegas right away. He says the fastest way is to fly from Elko to either Reno or Salt Lake on a feeder airline, and then take another flight to Vegas. I opt for Reno. I can leave this afternoon for Reno and take an early flight in the morning to Vegas. Sounds good to me. I now call, guess who—P.K.

"Hi, beautiful, got any plans for tonight and tomorrow night?"

Without any hesitation she responds, "I'm hoping to see a handsome lieutenant from Elko. Why do you ask?"

"Boy, you're good. Fast pick-up, baby."

"What's happening? Going back to Tahoe?"

"No, I've got to fly to Las Vegas tomorrow."

"You, in Las Vegas, without me? I don't think so."

I tell her what's going on and I'll be with the Vegas Metro cop all day.

"Two cops running around Vegas. That's supposed to make me feel better?"

"Honey, I'll be back in Reno by seven o'clock tomorrow night. Besides, you are the most beautiful woman in the world running around 'the biggest little city in the world' while I'm in the far side of the earth. You think I'm not worried?"

"Robert, I've told you, I've found what I want, you."

"Yeah, but another *me* could show up and sweep you off your feet. I hate you being so far away."

"Sweetheart, believe me, there is not another you. God broke the mold. One of you is all the world can handle. Don't be jealous of what isn't there. I want only you and me. We *will* work it out. I imagine you want me to pick you up tonight at the airport; right?"

"Please, around five or five-thirty. Whenever the puddle jumper finds Reno."

"I've heard horror tales about those planes. You make sure the pilot is sober before you let him fly."

The flight to Reno goes, uhh...well it goes. We finally make it. The ride is quite bumpy and the landing in Reno is a Disneyland E-ticket ride. Once Orville and Wilber get all the wheels to stay on the ground, the passengers, all six of us, cheer, offer prayers of thankfulness, etc.

A worried P.K. rushes up to me when I enter the terminal. After kisses and hugs she says, "I saw the landing. How many times did you bounce? I thought it was going to flip over."

"So did I. Let's move away from the door before the big guy who puked comes out. It was ugly."

We go home to P.K.'s. I feel "home" whenever I'm there. I feel "home" whenever I'm with her. Life is good. After dinner, we go to bed early as "somebody" must be at the airport early and "somebody else" must take me there. Good excuse as any.

P.K. leaves me at the airport with a warning. "You better be on the flight tonight, mister." She gives me "that look," then a big hug and long kiss. "Don't forget what you have here."

"How could I? You're the best thing that has happened to me, baby doll."

I land at Las Vegas McCarran Airport. Coming down the escalator into the arrival area a large black man wearing a tan sport coat, is holding a small handwritten sign: "CARSON." He looks like Danny Glover, but he's a real cop.

"What's with the sign?" I ask after shaking hands.

"The limo drivers use these to find their customers. I always wanted to try it. Worked like a charm. Here you are." He laughs. He is Preston, a homicide detective.

"Why homicide? Colton isn't dead, is he?"

"No, he's fine. The Chief of Investigations decided since this was involving one or more homicides, we should be involved."

Do I smell a turf war already? I hope not. This is too important to be petty.

Preston takes me to the Psychiatric Ward at UMC Hospital. He says Colton has become quite talkative, remembering a lot of his past.

We meet with Colton in a small room. He looks like he's been on drugs. Withered, worn out, bad teeth, all you would expect. I would not have recognized him on the street even if I had his old picture in my hand. I do have his photo and it's difficult. The eyes and nose are the same. The face is sunken, but the bone structure seems the same.

He looks at me. "What's the date?"

I tell him.

"Mom's birthday is coming up soon. I haven't called her for I don't know how long. Can I call her?"

What a breakthrough. The guy is back in this world.

He says to call him Dave. He then goes back to the beginning of his life on the streets. He had fooled around with some drugs, but nothing regular. One day at a truck stop in Mesquite, Nevada he was in the nearby casino when another driver comes up to him. He said the guy looked just like him. Could have been brothers. Was a southerner from Georgia, he remembers. They hit it off. Next thing he knows they're in his truck and "Bill" gives him some kind of drug.

"I don't remember what it was. It hit me big time. I was buzzed. It was great."

"What happened next?"

"I needed to get on my way and get my load delivered but I was too messed up to drive. Bill said he would drive me as far as Vegas. I went to sleep. I woke up a little while later and Bill pulled the truck over and said, "Here, take this. You'll feel better in the morning." I went out like a light. When I woke up, I was in a ditch alongside I-15 outside of Vegas. I climbed to the highway and couple of hippies stopped and offered me a ride. Also offered me some meth. That was it. I was hooked and all I wanted was more. They dropped me off in Vegas somewhere. I don't remember a lot of what I did after that. Just bits and pieces. I've been on the streets, homeless shelters, all of that. I even tried to clean up and get a job a few times. I always went back to the drugs. If that car hadn't hit me, I'd still be out there. Can I call my family? My mother? I'll even put up with my dad's religion. I want to be back in the world."

I tell Dave to go back to his room and I'll call his family.

"Thank you. I never said thank you to a cop before. Thank you."

Preston and I look at each other. Neither of us "hardened cops" have a dry eye. You don't get to witness this raw emotion often.

Preston and I go to Dave's treating doctor who's been standing by while we interview him. He's all for Dave going with family. The doctor said the accident was definitely a life saver. Dave was forced to go "cold turkey" and get his mind back. The doctor thinks he has a chance for recovery if he has the family's support.

We use his office to call the sister. She's beside herself with joy.

"I never expected to see him again, except at a funeral. Of course, he can come home. I'm a nurse. I'll see he makes it. Wait until I tell Mom. She won't believe it either."

"That answers my next question. Mom is still alive, I was hoping. I think that will make a difference to him. How will Dad be?"

"Dad died three years ago. Can I talk with David?"

We get the sister and David on the phone. It goes well. The sister will come out to Las Vegas and take him back to Illinois.

Before we leave, I ask Dave if he remembers telling Bill anything about his past. Where he was from, anything. He was sure he didn't. He renewed his CDL in Nebraska and used his employer's address for it. Apparently, a lot of drivers do that. So Weaton would not have any link to Illinois. I had explained to the sister why her brother's reappearance shouldn't be broadcast. Metro had already shut down the news after I said he would be a target.

Now it's time for me to fly to the arms of the one I love.

Preston takes me to the airport and manages to get me on an earlier flight. He's okay. He waits with me until it's time to leave. We talk about "*my case.*" He asks what I know about Weaton. I tell him about being from Georgia like Colton remembered, and he liked NASCAR.

"NASCAR's becoming a big thing here. In fact, there's a race in two weeks at the speedway."

"Two weeks. Weaton always tries to get his driving scheduled around big races."

"Why don't you come down about the middle of that week and we'll snoop around. Never know. We might find something."

"Sounds like a plan. I've got no other leads yet."

I call P.K. and tell her my new time. She's thrilled.

"You're spending the night, right?"

"If you'll have me?"

"You get on the plane." I love the sexy voice she can use.

P.K. is waiting for me when I get off the plane. After the hugs and kisses I look at her very seriously. "Hey baby, let's to go to Vegas."

"Right now?"

"No, actually the middle of next week, for a few days. There's a big NASCAR race and the metro detective and I think it might be worthwhile to poke around and see if we can find Weaton."

"And you wisely decided to ask me to go along. I'm proud of you, Robert; you just might make the grade."

"I wouldn't think of going without you."

"You are so full of it. Of course, I'll go. You're not going to run around with another cop in Vegas again."

"Preston is older, married, a genuinely good guy."

P.K. runs her fingers through my thinning hair. "Some could say *you* were *older,* and I think *you should be married.*"

"Yes, dear, could we go home now before we start to make out here in the terminal?"

Chapter36

Back in Elko, after getting George's approval for the next trip to Vegas, I brief the guys. They both want to "help," too. Sorry, guys, somebody must fight crime in this county.

I talk with Preston in Las Vegas about what we hope to do. He agrees it's a shot in the dark, but it seems like the best idea for now. He says there are a lot of places where truckers congregate on the east side of town near I-15 and the racetrack. He thinks we should just wander in and out of the area, casinos and truck stops. I tell him I won't be travelling alone.

"Hey, great cover. The two of us look too much like cops to be hanging around those places by ourselves. She doesn't look like a cop, does she?"

"Oh no. Blonde, beautiful, and petite."

"Good for you, Bob. I can meet you at the airport or are you getting a rental?"

"Oh yeah, definitely a rental. This is a mini vacation for us. Can you recommend a hotel that won't break the department's budget and yet be classy?"

"I can do even better. I have connections and I'll get you a preferred rate at one of the best hotels on the Strip."

The trip is set. The county will pay for my airfare and hotel and I'll pay for P.K.'s flight and the rental car. When I tell George about the plans, minus my travelling companion, he gives me a fatherly look. "Any chance you could take your lady along? It could be a nice trip for you two. It would be a shame to waste a Vegas trip and be by yourself."

"Well, that would be fun. I'll ask her and see if she can take off the time. Yes, great idea, George. Thank you."

"The county will pick up the rental car also. You've got to have a car down there. That place is just too big."

This is working out almost too well. Wait until I call P.K. She'll be thrilled. First class accommodations.

Later in the day when Gary's in the office, I ask him if he remembers anything else about Weaton. "The NASCAR fans are really big supporters of their favorite driver. Was he wearing a ball cap with a name or a number on it? Anything more you can remember could help. I know it was a long time ago."

"Believe me, boss, I've been racking my brain trying to think of anything to help out. He didn't wear a ball cap. He had on a cowboy hat. I remember it because it was different. It had feathers on the front of the crown. Like a peacock."

I know that hat. I get on my computer, go to the internet and before long I show Gary a picture of a race car driver with a hat just like he described.

"Yeah, yeah, that's it. How'd you know? Who is that guy?"

"Richard Petty. The 'King' of stock car racing. I may not hunt or fish, but I do know auto racing."

"The King, yeah, the King. That's who he said he liked. I thought it was a religious thing or something.

That's the hat."

"You know, Gary, you need to get out into the world more. There's more to life than chasing loose women in bars."

"How'd you know...I don't do that. Joseph, have you been telling stories about me?"

Joseph is laughing his ass off. "I think it's no secret you know every bartender and cocktail waitress in Elko County by their first name."

"It is how I get my sources, I'm an investigator; I have to know what's going on in the other side of life," he blusters defensively.

"Beware of the dark side, Luke," I say as I wander into my office.

In the evening I call the travelling companion who will keep me out of trouble. She is, of course, thrilled with the way it has worked out.

"Does George think it's time for you to settle down or is he just trying to keep his employee from making any embarrassing headlines? Oh, while I remember, I wanted to ask you if that poor guy, Colton, ever got to talk with his mother."

"Yes, he did. Preston told me the sister went to the mother's and they called. I guess it was pretty emotional from what the hospital told him."

"Good. He needed to talk with his mama."

"You are such the sweet thing, baby. You have a good heart."

"Aw, thank you; that's why we are so good together."

"Because opposites attract?"

"Yes, you are correct."

All is set. I'll be in Reno next Tuesday, and

Wednesday morning we both leave for Las Vegas. Looking forward to it. Yes, I need a vacation and *we* need to spend more time together. Win, win, I say.

The rest of the week drags by. Finally, it's time to travel. I get to Reno and the next day P.K. and I are boarding the plane for Las Vegas. An hour and fifteen minutes later we arrive at the Vegas airport. We get our rental car and drive to the hotel Preston has arranged for us. It's one of the *biggies* on the Strip. P.K. is wide-eyed and I am, too.

"Are you sure this is right?" she asks. "It doesn't look like a place a government employee should be staying."

"We'll find out soon enough," I reply as I pull into the valet parking for "Hotel Guests."

It *is* right. They have my reservation, and we are quickly taken to our room on the umpteenth floor. I guess I must tip the fawning little creep who takes us and our luggage to the room. Oh well, it is *Vegas,* and I don't want to look like a hick from the sticks. I pay him off and he leaves.

P.K. is standing by the window. "Honey, look at this view. I've seen pictures, but wow."

I walk over to her and put my arms around her. The view is impressive, I'll admit. We just stand there for a while. The big casino/hotels, the Strip, the mountains, impressive. This place is huge. I didn't realize how big Las Vegas was until now.

Our mood is jarred by my cell phone ringing. It's Preston from Metro. Time to get to work. *Oh yeah, the reason we're here.* He'll pick us up and we can go to some of the truck stops and casinos near I-15 where the truckers hang out.

We go down to the entrance and spot Preston's car. I introduce P.K. He says, "Yes, Bob, you were right. Beautiful lady. I'm pleased to finally meet you, P.K. When Bob came down before he wouldn't stop taking about his 'lady in Reno.'"

Bless you, Preston, you'll be on my Christmas card list.

P.K. blushes and thanks him. We go off to start our searching. On the way I tell Preston about the Richard Petty cowboy hat. He has seen them before.

"Do we stop anyone with the hat?" he laughs.

"This is where P.K. comes in quite handy. She knows 'eyes' as I've told you, but she's also particularly good at faces, bone structure, all that. She can even tell if a person's teeth are their own or not. Kind of scary, but a talented woman."

P.K. punches me in the shoulder.

The three of us go into the casino closest to the racetrack. It's decorated with checkered flags, banners for the race, and of course, sponsors' products, usually beer. We wander around. Yep, this is truckers' world. They're all wearing hats. There's a baseball hat for every driver there ever was. A few cowboy hats but no Petty cowboy hats, so we also look for the "King's" ball caps. No one under them even remotely resembles Weaton. We move on to more casinos and I keep P.K. close to me. She's looking *much too good* for these places. By the end of the afternoon, we have pretty much covered the area near the track. Preston says by evening the crowds will have picked up considerably. The locals will start coming in. By now I am starting to think we are looking for a *needle* in a *needle stack.*

Next, we cruise the area's truck stops. We go in

and out of the coffee shops, lounge areas, etc. P.K. draws much too much interest in these places. Preston and I could be buck naked, and no one would notice. At least we get them all to look up at us. No Weaton. P.K. is a real trooper. She studies their faces intently. I don't think they're looking entirely at her face. "She had a face?" I can hear them if asked.

"No more truck stops unless we get you a muumuu and a sunbonnet."

"I'm okay; it's sort of fun to look at all the faces searching for Weaton's features. Lots of bad teeth I will say. But you two stay close."

By early evening, Preston suggests we knock off and resume the following afternoon. He takes us back to the hotel and suggests several restaurants and sights for us to check out. We do. We have a fabulous dinner in our hotel's steak house and then walk the Strip. We check out the water shows, Pirate Ship battle, take a gondola on the canals of Venice. We wear ourselves out being tourists. Great fun. Great companion. I don't want this to end.

Next day, same scenario. In and out of all the trucker and race fan hangouts. No Petty hats. No Weaton we can spot. In all honesty he could be right behind us half the time. There are so many people.

During dinner at the NASCAR Café, P.K. says, "You said Richard Petty isn't driving anymore. Maybe 'Wheaties' has a new driver to support. You do."

She should have been a cop, but she's too nice. Sometimes her logic scares me. Of course, he'd have a new driver to root for. Yes, I lost my favorite and chose his replacement to follow. I definitely have to keep this woman around, in spite of her insisting on using the cereal for my suspect's name.

The three of us leave the Strip and go to Fremont Street, the original Vegas tourist area. Located there is Race Rock Café which is, as the name says, a race-themed establishment. It's extra crowded. Since P.K. is shorter than Preston or I, we keep her between us. I hang onto her hand. All of a sudden, she yanks my hand. I look at her. With her eyes she points at the man right next to her. He's moving toward the bar.

"What about him?" I lean down as the place is very noisy.

"What was Petty's racecar number?"

"Uh, 43."

"That guy has a red and blue '43' tattoo on his arm."

He's now standing at the bar trying to get a drink. I tell Preston so we all try to maneuver to get nearer. The place is so crowded we can't get close enough to see him. P.K., determined she's right, slips out of my hand and steps in front of two other customers with an "Excuse me, fellas." Gets right alongside the man. She looks up at him and I can see by the change in her face that it's not him. She squeezes back to us.

"Not him; darn, right height, too."

I grab her hand and almost drag her outside. Preston's laughing.

"Bob, you got yourself a winner with her. P.K., please don't do that again, though; we could have lost you in that crowd."

"Yes, please don't do that again. But good eye."

"I had to see. You two couldn't get through without starting a fight," she says smugly.

We are done for the day. The happy couple become

tourists again and enjoy the sights of Vegas.

On Friday, the first of the races at the Las Vegas Motor Speedway begins.

Preston says, "It will be useless for us to go anywhere near the track itself, because the traffic becomes gridlocked. The truck stops are becoming packed, more everyday as the weekend nears. Evidently, your Weaton isn't the only one who arranges his schedule around races. Let's make one final sweep of the eastside casinos and call it good. I think it's a highly unlikely maneuver, but let's make a valiant effort anyway."

I've learned I have a valuable new team member, if I can keep her under close watch.

"No more *solo* missions."

"Yes, Lieutenant Carson." She salutes me.

We have Friday evening and all of Saturday to ourselves. We say goodbye to Preston, and he tells us the next time we come down, we'll have to go to dinner with his wife and him. Sounds nice. I like him. P.K. likes him, too.

We go up to our room. It has, of course, been made up while we were gone. There's some new "literature" on the table from the hotel. There are always little cards about their restaurants, spas, gyms etc. but this time on top is one for their "wedding chapel." We both see at it at the same time. The brochure is done up quite nicely. Very classy, in fact. No waiting, same day weddings, licenses, witnesses all provided. Start your life together in Las Vegas, it says.

We look at each other. Eyes meet and we melt together.

"What do you think?" I say.

"We don't need a big formal wedding." She's beaming.

I go to my suitcase, remove something, and go back to her. Ever the consummate gentleman, I drop to one knee, take her hand, and look into her beautiful eyes. "P.K., will you marry me?" I produce a diamond engagement ring. I bought the ring when I was in the Tahoe jewelry store at Christmas. I've kept it with me waiting for the right time. Hoping it would come. Now it has.

She gently pulls me up, throws her arms around me, and says softly, "Yes, Robert, I will."

From then on, our emotions run wild. We cannot stop hugging, kissing, laughing, and yes, even crying. It's a memory I will cherish the rest of my life.

"It's exquisite, Robert. I love it!" She holds up her hand with the ring on. "When did you get it?"

"In Tahoe where I got your Christmas present."

"You were thinking marriage even before our first Christmas together? Honestly, you were not the only one. I felt a strong bond forming between us. One that would last a lifetime. Why did you wait so long to ask me?"

"I wanted to be sure you were certain about us."

"You had me hooked at the first date. But yes, we did have to see how it all worked out. And boy, did it work out." She puts a soft hand on each side of my face and draws me in for a lengthy passionate kiss.

Catching my breath, I say, "Yes it did, my love. Now let's find out how this wedding chapel thing works."

I discover in Vegas everything is available any time of the day or night. If we come down to the chapel, they'll get us to the 24-hour city marriage license office and then we can get whatever kind of wedding we want. They have small, medium, and large wedding plans. They'll supply witnesses, cake, photos, even guests if we want some. Only in Vegas.

We look at each other. We want to do this, but we want an intimate wedding to bind us together. Not a commercial thing.

Then my cell rings. It's Preston.

"Hey, guys, I just got home and was telling my wife about our day. She said why wait for your next trip. If you don't already have plans, how about dinner tonight?"

"Uh...well, we...uh...actually we were looking at the hotel's wedding chapel and thinking about getting married tonight." I blurt this all out because my head is still spinning. I'm excited. I'm giddy. I feel like a little kid.

Preston gets quiet. "Listen, Bob, you don't want to get married in one of those glitzy places, do you? I have a better idea. We were married years ago in this little wedding chapel on the south end of the Strip. It looks like a little country church. The staff is made up of real people, not hyped-up sales types. My wife and I would be honored to be your witnesses and then take you out to dinner as a wedding present. What do you say?"

P.K., with her bat-like hearing, has heard it all. She nods enthusiastically at me.

"You sure about this, Preston? That's quite nice of you and your wife."

Mrs. Preston apparently has bat-like hearing also. Must be a female trait.

"Hello, Bob. Preston has told me all about you and

your lovely lady. Preston is right. You do not want to go to one of those cheesy hotel places. This wedding chapel is charming. Put your lady, P.K. is it, on the phone."

I hand the phone to P.K. and they talk like they've known each other for years.

When they're done P.K. puts down the phone. "What a wonderful lady. They will pick us up in an hour downstairs. Let's get dressed up." Then she kisses me. "This still okay with you?"

"Let's do it." I grab her and we kiss more.

"Robert, they're on their way; we need to get dressed." She giggles, giving me a gentle shove. "Plenty of time later."

We go with Preston and his wife Marie to the marriage license office, then on to the chapel.

"Oh, honey, it's enchanting," says the soon-to-be Mrs. Carson.

It is charming. Like a tiny church you would find nestled in the hills among the pine trees. Only it's on the edge of the Strip. Not surrounded by casinos...at least not yet. The way Las Vegas is growing it won't be long, sadly.

Preston has called ahead, and all is arranged. We've hit a good time and don't even have to wait. Marriage is a steady business in Vegas.

Priscilla Killarney Kelly is radiant in a cream-colored cocktail dress she packed in case we went to see a star-studded show. In my eyes it is the perfect wedding gown. She couldn't be more radiant and beautiful. I am somewhat dapper in blue blazer and slacks. The minister does not look like Elvis, as is the vogue here. He is pastoral in demeanor.

The ceremony is everything we could have hoped for. It felt as though the cleric knew what was in our hearts and spoke with an understanding of the vows we wanted to express to one another. Slipping the ring on her finger I felt my heart would beat out of my chest. I've never been so happy. We are now *husband and wife.*

A couple of photos and Mr. and Mrs. Carson are off to dinner with their witnesses. I thank Preston and his wife profusely for the suggestion.

Marie leans over and takes P.K.'s arm. "You two deserve to get the right start. You'll be fine."

The evening with our friends passes in a blur of toasts and laughter. I'm certain no one has had more fun at a reception than the four of us. We will be friends for life.

Back at the hotel we settle in for our first night as a married couple. The first of many, many happy nights.

Chapter 37

We sleep in late the next morning. Then it's a leisurely brunch overlooking the canals of Venice. When we're finished my bride says, "Let's go over to those shops we saw on the way in." She leads me around a corner and into a jeweler.

"You're not going back to Elko *unclaimed.* I'll go to my favorite jeweler when we get back to Reno. But for now, I want you to have a ring. Besides, I've been sketching a special design for you."

"You mean you thought I would eventually propose?"

"I was hoping." She grabs me and gives me a big hug.

She finds a "suitable" ring for now. A rather hefty gold band with some carving. Nothing cheap about this lady.

"This is a *temporary* ring? Baby, this is beautiful. Good thing it's not my gun hand. It would throw off my aim," I joke as she puts it on my finger.

The jeweler backs off and his hand goes under the counter. Searching for his panic button, I suspect. "It's okay, I'm a police officer."

He relaxes. "Of course, sir."

Outside after we stop laughing about the poor jeweler. I tell *my wife,* "This is a fine piece of jewelry, but I have you, I don't need anything more."

"You're getting a 'P.K.' designed ring and that's that."

"Yes, ma'am."

On the plane back to Reno Sunday morning, we talk about our upcoming life together. P.K. will make her first trip to Elko as soon as she can arrange her schedule. She juggled some patients to make the Vegas trip, so she will be tied up for a couple of weeks.

"How's your brother going to take this?" I finally ask. I like the big guy, but I know he adores his *little sister.*

"He'll be fine. He approves of you. You're the first guy I've dated in a long time he likes. His wife will be a little miffed we didn't have a fancy wedding, but she'll get over it."

"Maybe she wanted to be the maid of honor?"

"You got it. She never said so, but that's what I think. It'll be fine."

Since I don't have to leave until Monday (Orville & Wilbur don't fly on Sunday), we decide to stop at the brother's when we get into Reno and break the news.

"Oh, you guys." He has a big grin. "I thought you might do that given a chance. It's a little early, but I've got some champagne. Let's have a toast."

His wife is great about it. Maybe she didn't want to be the maid of honor after all.

"To the Carsons. May they be as *happy* as we are." He raises his glass. We all do the same and take a sip of "early morning champagne."

"I knew you were right for my sister, Bob. I have never seen her as happy as when she started dating you. I like your crazy sense of humor. It's good for her, too. Brings out a side of her I haven't seen enough of."

I start to get misty-eyed. P.K. squeezes my hand. Nice to have his approval.

Chapter 38

The Wright brothers manage to get me safely back to Elko and I go straight to the office. My crew is waiting for me. All smiles and asking about the trip. I don't detect any nervousness, so I presume they stayed out of trouble.

They did.

Joseph stares at my left hand.

"What's that? Let me see. Is that what I think it is? You guys got hitched, didn't you?"

"A ring. Here, look. Yes, it is. Yes, we did get married. Any more questions?" I wave my left hand around for all to see and admire my finery.

"Good, now you're settled. I'm doing great with my new lady, so all we need now is to get some lonely schoolteacher for Gary."

"Why a schoolteacher?"

"Because they're about the only profession you haven't gone through in the county."

"I haven't met any."

"That's because they don't hang out in bars."

We then get down to work. The guys have been doing their job and I have no concerns. Several messages are waiting for me.

First on my list is the Arizona Highway Patrol Captain. He received several "hits" on Weaton's DNA from CODIS (Combined DNA Index System), the FBI's nationwide registry of samples entered into the system. His DNA shows up on various unsolved cases around the country. Most are dead women, who, like my cases, are found alongside the highway. Two are women who survived; they described a southern man with Weaton Colton-like names as the assailant. One was Al and the other was Randy. This would be Weaton's middle name of Randall. The captain had forwarded the photos to the reporting agencies. The victims each picked one of the "disguised" pictures as the responsible party. This means they were committed after Weaton took over Colton's ID.

As far as the homicide cases go, there is little, or no evidence of the perpetrator as has been the case in the past. Bodies dumped in the middle of the night on some lightly travelled portion of a highway. The Captain and I try to contact as many trucking associations as we can find to alert them to Weaton's *newest* identity: Earnest William Bennett, the poor guy whose body was found hanging off the culvert on the Arizona highway. I have updated my now famous *Truck Stop Flyer* with Bennett's name and info.

Why Weaton didn't keep Bennett's truck and continue the job is only speculation. There was some reason he didn't continue with the company. Leaving the blood-spattered tractor was not a wise move. It's a mistake which will eventually bring him to justice. We now have his DNA, and it matches several homicides.

Weaton is now *Bennett* with a valid CDL, and his name plastered all over the country, trying to get a truck driving job. What would he do under these circumstances? Some criminologists would suggest contacting a behavioral psychologist for this kind of a case.

I prefer to go to the real experts: actual truckers.

I start to hang out in the local truck stops again. I'm on a first-name basis now. It's still amazing to me how fast this news spreads throughout the field. These guys seem to be hooked up better than law enforcement. With their CB radios and now cell phones they know what's going on all over the country's roadways.

I talk with a lot of drivers in the ensuing days. The consensus of opinion is since he's a loner, Weaton will try to stay with a long-haul trucking firm, but a small one. A company that is not a member of a national association of truckers. He's trying to stay under the radar. There are apparently lots of small trucking firms around serving regional areas.

The drivers' logic makes sense to me. Weaton's past has been basically West-East routes. His victims have been near interstate highways. If he now switches to the North-South routes, ones he hasn't traveled too much in the past, he has a better chance of not being noticed.

The drivers all want to grab a handful of the updated flyers and pass them out on their routes. An advantage to being in Elko is a lot of the North-South guys pass through here going to Idaho and on to Washington, even to Canada.

Canada.

I hadn't thought much about Canada. It brings in border crossings. If he must deliver in Canada, he'll pass through Customs and Border Patrol check points. The drivers tell me it's very common for the northern area truckers to cross back and forth between the U.S.

and Canada.

Time to call FBI Andy.

Andy is, as always, glad to assist. Somehow, he'll get credit when the capture is made. That's the FBI way. He'll call whomever he must in order to get this information to the CBP (Customs and Border Patrol). Getting this information to the CBP will also alert the U.S./Mexico check points.

Now it's time to sit back and wait again. Fortunately, there are always plenty of local cases to handle.

In between I get my modest abode ready for P.K.'s upcoming visit. I'm nervous. I want it to be perfect. Yes, she has already married me, so some of the pressure is off, but I still want to impress her as to how responsible I am. The house and yard are both perfect. I have the sore back to prove it. I stocked up on food. Real food, not the frozen stuff I usually have on hand. If I can con her into cooking, I'm home free. I can BBQ, but my indoor talents are limited.

Other than me, no one is happier to have me married than my neighbors, Mary and Fred. A genuinely nice, retired couple. They've been worried about me dying a lonely old bachelor since I moved in. They are truly good neighbors. Because of my irregular hours they keep an eye on my place. No one makes a better watchdog than retired people. They don't mind having a *cop* next door either.

It's now time for P.K. to come home. I like the sound of that, home with me. She has her appointments up-to-date and will have a few days to see her future home. Scary, I hope she can adjust to Elko. It's not Reno.

She has her eyes open. She tells me, "I go where you go."

Love this woman.

She wants to drive but I won't hear of it. Too long a trip on an isolated highway for a woman alone. I'll drive to her and bring her back. That's that.

And I do.

During the ride she agrees it's a long, long barren road.

We drive her Jeep "Baby" as the Porsche doesn't have enough room for milady's *needs* for the trip. To be honest, it doesn't have much room for even my meager needs for more than a couple of days.

We pull up to my house and she's delighted. "It's cute. You made it sound like a dump. I like it."

So far, so good.

Inside she continues to be pleased. Punching the pillows on the couch into the proper shape and appraising the furniture I have managed to acquire. I can feel the mental decorating going on in her head.

"Robert, you sold this place short. It's quite nice. Yes. I like it. We'll be extremely happy here." She says, like a pronouncement of our forthcoming life...

Then I get a thought. *Why hadn't I thought of it first?*

"Come back outside in the front." I almost drag her.

Outside the front door I stop and turn around and scoop her up and *carry her across the threshold* into *our* home.

P.K. puts her arms around my neck and begins to cry. "I love you," she says. "I love this home, our home."

217

Chapter 39

The next night I plan to take P.K. to a local restaurant I like. "Not your brother's place, but it's good."

"As long as we're together it will be grand."

"That's nice, Baby, but wait until you see Elko. You've only seen the edge."

I drive through "town." It only takes a few minutes. Old, older, and a few new strip malls on the outskirts.

To her credit P.K. does not jump out of the car screaming and run for the freeway. She appears to like the area.

"Don't forget Reno has old and new, too," she lectures. "It's a slice of Nevada history."

Cuddled close together in a booth at the restaurant, we enjoy a well-prepared dinner. It helps I prepped the owner, and a small wedding cake is delivered to our table with a flourish and good wishes from the staff. It brings tears to her eyes.

Good start, Robert.

The next day we tour more of the area. The nearby Ruby Mountains are stunning. She loves them. In fact, she wants to paint them. She's a talented artist, remember. I avoid some of the more controversial parts of the county. No sense overloading her. Besides, Undersheriff George and his wife have invited us over for dinner. They're gracious and welcome P.K. into the family. It doesn't matter where you are, law enforcement is a close-knit group.

Before we leave, George's wife gets me aside. "Oh, Bob, she's so sweet. I like her. You be good to her." I keep hearing this from everyone's wife, geez. *Like I wouldn't be?*

As we're leaving, George's wife tells P.K. "Call me if you need any help getting settled and I want to see your painting of the Ruby Mountains when it's finished. I have always loved the Ruby Mountains, but I've never had a painting of them. I think it's time."

"I'm flattered, but you haven't seen my work yet."

"Well yes, dear, I have. I've seen the painting you made for Bob...*Robert*...for his office. The *Gathering Storm,* I believe. It genuinely catches the mood of an impending thunderstorm. Yes, I would love you to do a painting of the Rubys for me."

My little artist is thrilled. "I like them, especially her. I can't wait to start my painting."

Monday morning I'm going to take the new Mrs. Carson to the office to meet my crew. I offer to come back and get her at a more decent time than eight a.m., but she says she'll come in with me. We walk in the office and the guys are "looking good," fresh, and professional. *Thank you, boys.*

Joseph is his gracious self. Gary manages not to drool, as I had half expected him to. My P.K. is an attractive lady and his eyes are wide open for a change. Not normal for eight in the morning for him. Good boy, Gary.

I show her around the office and introduce her to everyone.

She's well received. I'm happy.

She is relieved. "I've been so nervous about meeting all your friends and co-workers. They've been so accepting of me and everyone seems to genuinely like you."

"Why should that surprise you? I'm a nice guy."

Back in my office I remind my people, "I'm taking you guys and my bride to dinner tonight. Joseph, you invite your lady and Gary, do you have anyone you would like to bring along to a "family" dinner?

Joseph rolls his eyes.

"As a matter of fact, I've been seeing a lady even Joseph would approve of. We'll be there," Gary says with an indignant huff.

"You guys were awfully hard on Gary." P.K. says as we leave the office. "But I can tell he thinks he's a real lady's man."

"As long as he behaves himself around you that's all that matters. Yes, he does believe God put him on this earth for the ladies. He just hasn't found any *ladies* yet."

At the restaurant, Joseph, his new lady love, P.K., and I are already seated when in walks Gary. On his arm is an attractive, well dressed woman. She's around Gary's age. Not his typical type of female, I admit. Joseph's mouth almost hits the table. We're introduced to his date. Everyone wants to talk at once. We're nosey. It turns out she's a youth counselor for the county. Perfect. This woman is used to dealing with troubled youths. Exactly what Gary needs. Someone who understands him. Met Gary through the job and not at a bar. Now I understand why his eyes have been clear in the mornings. She's a lot of fun and we share a good, lively dinner.

The remainder of the week we hang out at my place—now our place—or take rides throughout the county. We go to the Ruby Mountains and I take photos for her of areas she would like to paint. She's getting into the locale.

Thank you, God.

She says she could move her business to Elko. "Most of my patients need to travel to see me anyway. They come from all around Nevada and adjoining states. There are not a lot of ocularists, so I think it won't hurt my business to move. Let's look for possible office locations."

"There are some new office buildings near the hospital." We check them out and find one perfect for her. It's not too big. She only needs a couple of rooms. Back at home, we discuss it.

"I like it. It's just right for me. Let's scoop it up before someone else does."

"You're sure?"

"I told you, Robert; you're here so I'm here. Done deal."

We *scoop it up.*

She can take possession by the next week. The owner is so happy to fill the space he offers to paint the walls whatever color she wants.

"I can move here now, huh?" she coyly looks at me. We make our plans for the "Great Move." Then we go crazy; what about this, what about that. It's wild and weird. Two kids on a new adventure. We decide she'll keep her home in Reno. She should. It's lovely and in a great neighborhood. For the present we'll use it to store all her *stuff* that won't fit into my place, which brings up another point. We should buy a house. Now this is getting complicated. I hate dealing with realtors.

"Not to worry," she smiles. "Before I became an ocularist I was a realtor. I know the business. I can deal with them."

Is there nothing this woman of mine can't do?

George refers us to a realtor he's known for years.

"She's a pit bull. She'll eat another realtor's liver to make a sale."

P.K. nods approvingly at this revelation. "That's the kind of realtor we want."

And I thought police work was tough.

The lady shows us some homes for sale in our price range that meet our needs. They're nice, but none with the *wow* factor we are hoping for. We're a little discouraged. We decide to wait a while. My wife still needs to move here and get her business up and running. We are going to be together. That's all that matters.

I take Mrs. Carson back to Reno. This is harder than ever. After a full week together, we don't want to be separated. The first order of business is to get her office moved to Elko. Then we can work on housing. I'm thinking we can rent a truck and move her office stuff and some of her personal belongings ourselves. She agrees. P.K. will start to do what she must to move her business to Elko. The physical moving is not the big part. She'll need to advise the doctors who refer patients to her and her established patients of her new practice.

Insensitively I ask, "How many eyes do they need? Why would they come back?" Then I remember Weaton. "Oh duh, for replacements, huh?" The brilliant investigator has now totally embarrassed himself.

"I also do cleaning and adjustments for my people," I am told.

The matter solved; we agree she'll need at least a week to get everyone notified. Upon checking her schedule, P.K. realizes it will take at least two or three more weeks before she can switch patients to Elko.

As I'm kissing her good-bye, she looks at me with those gorgeous eyes. "It won't be too long. At least we now have a time frame. You go catch Wheaties."

Chapter 40

Back in Elko it's business as usual. Then in the middle of the week I get a phone call from a trucker at one of the local truck stops. He asks if he can see me.

You bet. I'll be right there. If a trucker wants to talk to me, I bet it's about Wheaties. *Damn,* now she has me doing it.

I meet the trucker in the coffee shop, where else? He has just travelled from Portland, Oregon en route to Denver.

"While I was waiting to fuel up in Portland, I chatted with another driver. He had a distinct southern accent, was asking about the action in the area. He was referring to the bar scene and availability of women.

"Said he was new to the northwest trucking scene. It meant nothing to me at the time. But when I got to Idaho, I saw a recent flyer at a truck stop. It mentions Weaton may be travelling in the northwest area. The more I thought about the meeting, the more I thought it could be Weaton. This guy had long blond hair—almost to his shoulders—and a scraggly mustache."

I show him my various pictures.

"That has to be him. The messed up left cheek is the giveaway." His finger is resting on the newest rendition of the Wheaton faces.

Now I ask all kinds of questions. What company was he driving for? Where was he going? Did he talk about his personal life? Anything to help track him down.

"Well, the tractor was a Hertz rental. Ya know companies use them when they need extra units. A name was taped onto the cab, but I didn't get close enough to read it. Had no reason to. I was in the fuel line ahead of him, I didn't see a name on the trailer. But I can tell ya it was a *reefer,* a refrigerated enclosed trailer used for transporting perishables. Bill, the name he gave me, was hauling apples from the packing house to the distributors. This trip he was heading to South San Francisco, to the produce market."

Bill (William) is Weaton's first name and Bennett's middle.

I ask, "What else was talked about?"

"Besides wanting to know where the women of the area could be found, he asked about car racetracks. Said he was a big fan and hoped to go to one of the NASCAR races in California this season. He'd been at the Las Vegas Speedway and loved it."

Damn! I knew it. He was there. I'm sick inside, I feel my body go rigid. Taking a deep breath and releasing it before I continue questing him, I ask, "Exactly when were you in Portland and at which truck stop?"

The driver gives me his logbook. It has the entry date, as well as the receipt for fuel. He tells me Weaton would have been the next one to use the pump.

"I need you to come with me to my office and give a brief written statement and let me copy the logbook entry and receipt."

"Sure, but where am I going to park my rig in town?"

"I'll drive you to the police station and bring you back to the truck stop."

"Okay, as long as you bring me back. I've stayed in a couple of jails before and didn't like them." He laughs.

I bring him to the office, and he gives a good statement. This will be helpful for probable cause if I need a search warrant for the truck stop's records. Usually not a problem, but at this stage of the game I'm taking no chances. I return the driver to his rig and thank him again for his help.

Now it's back to the undersheriff. He agrees I need to go to Portland in person and follow this up quickly. He arranges with the Portland P.D. for assistance and has my flight booked.

Oh Lord, Orville and Wilbur again. *K.P. is not going to like this.*

"Can't you just drive there?" she asks. "I'd feel safer."

"No, baby, time is of the essence."

"Time isn't going to matter if you're wrapped around a pine tree in Oregon."

"You think I'll make it that far?"

"Stop it, Robert. I'm being serious. Remember the last trip to Reno? Please check out those guys before you take off."

"I'll make them walk the white line down the center of the runway."

She sighs. "I married a smart-ass, but I knew it going in."

Getting to Portland is not a simple thing. My choices are Elko to Salt Lake City or Elko to Phoenix, then on to Portland. No direct flights. It's a two- to five-hour trip depending on which flight you pick. Driving looks better every minute, but flying it is.

I arrive at the Elko airport and see a larger plane than last time, which will take me to Salt Lake City. Orville and his brother are not around; instead, it's Susan and Bernice. Yes, both pilots are ladies. And boy, they can fly. Best trip I've had in some time. Smooth landing in Utah. After a forty-five-minute layover, I find my connecting flight. I get on board with two male pilots who make Orville and Wilbur look good. But they handle the plane as smoothly as the ladies did.

I arrive in the late afternoon and I'm met by a Portland detective, Lou. He takes me straight to the truck stop. No problem with the management; we get the information on the truck that fueled up right after my informant's truck.

Yes, indeed, the driver signed the receipt as E. Bennett. The fuel was charged to a local trucking firm that hauls fresh produce to market.

"I've handled cases of theft reported by this company," Lou says. "Let's go to the trucking company's main office. It's nearing six p.m. but hopefully, some management is still around."

The owner is there. He's a no-nonsense guy. Built up the business from one truck to a fleet of twenty. Business is good now since the produce is ripe and needs to get to the consumer.

"Yes, I rent tractors during this time of year and yes, Bennett's a new hire. I didn't check him out as thoroughly as I could have, I admit. I didn't check with former employers like I usually do. I needed drivers. The guy was personable and had all he needed: current

CDL and medical card. He was able to back up the rig without hitting anything, so I hired him." After checking with his dispatcher, he says "Bennett made his delivery in South San Francisco and is on his way back to Portland. He is deadheading, meaning no return load. Should be back late tomorrow."

The only people who know we're here are the owner and the dispatcher. We impress upon the owner how important it is to keep it that way. Bennett/Weaton must have no hint we are here asking questions. The owner declares his dispatcher has been with him for years and will make sure nothing is said.

Lou calls his captain and tells him what we have found out. The Portland P.D. has already received a copy of my warrants for Weaton; no legal problems there. Portland will supply detectives to assist us when Weaton pulls into the yard. Marked patrol units will be nearby but kept out of sight.

Is this the end of the hunt? Can it be this easy...after all this time?

I call Undersheriff George and bring him up to date. He's so excited he wants to come up to Portland. But he can't, the sheriff's on vacation. George is stuck in Elko. Fine with me. This is *my* show. *I* started it and *I* want to finish it.

Lou gets me to my hotel and suggests dinner. Don't these guys have a life away from the job? Oh yeah, look who is talking. I was there myself, not too long ago. I'll call P.K., then meet him at the restaurant down the street.

"Honey, you be careful. You have waited too long for this. Don't get careless."

"I promise. This will be by the book."

I go to meet Lou. I'll call my bride again after dinner. I need to talk with her tonight. She gives me comfort.

Chapter 41

I have trouble sleeping. Can this be the conclusion of the chase? It has been such a long, twisted path to get to this point. My emotions are ranging up and down. I think of the pain, horror, and grief this man has caused his victims and their families. It needs to end tomorrow; it must.

I call P.K. again. The third time tonight. She told me to call if I needed to talk more. The woman can see inside me, I swear.

We talk more and then she says, "Please try to sleep. You need be at your best tomorrow. I want you to be with me, forever."

How did I find her? It's like it was fated. I believe it was.

I manage some sleep.

At seven a.m. my cell phone rings. It's Joseph.

"Hey, Boss, you know how I get those *feelings?* Well, they're saying *you need to be very careful today. It's not going to go down easy."*

"What do you mean, exactly?

"You know about my owl. I saw him, I don't know, just flying back and forth. Like he was nervous or agitated. He was not calm like he usually is. I felt I had to warn you to be alert. I...uhh...we need you back, Lieutenant. Be careful, please."

"Thank you, Joseph; I appreciate your concern. I'll

be by the book."

Lou from Portland PD picks me up and we go to his station. We call the trucking company owner, who says he has heard nothing so far from Weaton/Bennett. His last call said he'd be at the freight yard early this afternoon.

Lou's captain meets us and assigns two detectives to assist us. He has planned with the patrol captain to have at least two marked units available when we're ready to move.

Not much to do for now. I suggest to Lou we go to the company and hang out, just in case. He agrees. He's as anxious as I am. Remembering how bad the coffee pot in the freight office smelled, we grab some Starbucks and head over. As we walk in the door the owner has the phone in his hand. He puts it down. "I was about to call you guys. Bennett checked in and should be here in about an hour. He told the dispatcher he's partying tonight and is in a hurry to get back."

"Does he have a place here in Portland?" I ask. Weaton never seems to hang his hat anywhere.

"Yeah, he has an apartment a few blocks from here. Our drivers are home a lot. Some of the runs don't take too long, not like the long haulers. Bennett said he was ready to settle down."

He gives us the address of the apartment. After Lou calls his captain to get the other units alerted, we decide to check out the apartment. It's close. Lou says we can go and be back in ten minutes.

A misty rain is falling as we head out. Rain's the norm up here, I'm told. The apartment building is a modest two-story place. No room to park a big rig, the building is too close to the street. Weaton's apartment is on the top floor in the front of the building. No activity so we head back to the trucking yard. When the other detectives arrive, we pull all our cars behind the main office, out of sight. The marked patrol units are to wait down the street behind some offices, also out of sight.

Everyone is ready. This is always the worst part of an operation. Just waiting. Then the dispatcher's phone rings, and we all jump.

Edgy? Not us.

The dispatcher answers, then looks at us and puts his finger to his lips. He has a brief conversation and says to the caller, "Okay, Bill, take it easy; be your usual charming self, and we'll see you when you get in."

He hangs up and turns to us. "Bill just got pulled over by Highway Patrol for speeding. He's about five miles away on the freeway. He seemed alright about it. Said he was only going five over."

Damn Highway Patrol must do their job. Rain and all.

We debate our next move. The Interstate is busy this time of day and the Portland boys think trying to move in on him now would endanger too many civilians. Not to mention the officers on the rain-slicked highway. This is a tough call. We decide to contact the HP dispatcher and advise them of our interest in the trucker and ask if they can contact the officer. Call him off on some ruse, so Weaton can leave. Lou makes the call. The Highway Patrol dispatcher agrees and calls the officer in question. Lou listens intently. A couple of minutes go by.

"He's not answering. She's called his number several times. She's now advising all units in the area to check on the officer," Lou whispers while still listening.

How long has it been since Weaton called in? Almost ten minutes, says the trucking dispatcher.

Lou asks the highway patrol dispatcher, "Did the officer call in a check for wants on the driver?"

The dispatcher says she hasn't heard from him since he radioed in he was making the stop. Something's wrong. This is not a usual stop. Lou is still on the phone and another highway patrol unit, travelling on the opposite side of the interstate, radios in he sees the patrol car on the side of the road. No sign of the officer or a truck.

I look at the trucking company owner. "Does he have a car?"

"Yes, a Chevy pickup. He leaves it at his apartment."

I take charge; I can't help it. "Lou, we need to go to the apartment. You guys stay here in case he shows up." The detectives nod agreement.

Lou's car slips and slides as he drives swiftly out of the wet parking lot. "You think he's on to us?"

"No, but something happened at the traffic stop and I don't think it was good."

The Portland PD radio advises the highway patrol officer has been located. He's been shot.

I knew it...*I just knew it!*

We come sliding around the corner to Weaton's apartment. On the street in front of the apartment is his truck. Running toward the apartment is a man wearing a NASCAR jacket and carrying a small suitcase. Lou speeds up and turns to cut him off. I bail out with weapon in hand. The man spins and starts to run the other way.

"Weaton, it's over! Freeze, put your hands up!"

He stops, drops the suitcase, and unhurriedly raises his hands over his head.

"On the ground—Now!"

Weaton starts to move like he's going to kneel and then turns his left side toward me, with his left hand still in the air. As he's turning, he drops his right hand toward his waist under the jacket.

"Don't do it. Raise your hand or I'll shoot you!"

What happens next is like slow motion. He keeps reaching under his jacket and I see a gun in his hand. He starts to point it toward me.

I fire two quick shots. Weaton shudders, then drops to his knees. He still has the gun.

"Drop the gun!"

He tries to raise it again, then he falls on his side. As his head smashes to the ground his false eye slips out and rolls onto the rain-soaked pavement.

The eye on the side of the road started this pursuit and now on the side of the road the eye ends it.

Chapter 42

Weaton's one eye flutters. He starts to squirm. I kick the gun away from him. Lou is there and picks it up.

"Bob, nice shooting."

"Actually, I want the bastard alive." My insides feel like I'm on fire. I want so badly to grab him and scream in his face, why?

"I'm hurt; get me to a hospital," Weaton wails.

"You didn't seem to care about the women you hurt: the ones in Oklahoma, Nevada, two in California, or any of the others around the country. And what about poor Bennett and Colton?" I spit back at him.

"There wa–was only one in Ca-California. Only…uh…one." He's starting to fade.

Our backup and paramedics arrive.

"Looks like he has a sucking chest wound," I tell the paramedic.

"Yeah, that's what it looks like to me," he agrees after examining Weaton. "Those are painful. We'll get him to the hospital right away."

"Make sure you don't miss any potholes," I say under my breath, as I walk away.

The shooting team from Portland P.D. has also arrived. They will conduct their own investigation, as it's an officer-involved shooting. I let Lou talk to them first. I go over to his car and sit down.

It's time to call the woman who holds my soul.

The phone stops ringing, and I start to speak. My voice is met with racking sobs. Oh God. I forget how hard it is on the people who love us. When law enforcement personnel are in the field, we become so intent on what we are doing—plans, safety, adrenalin, what ifs—we become our own world. We forget the wives, husbands, and children who, no matter what they're doing, are wrapped in an invisible blanket of terror. When will the phone ring? What if it doesn't?

I begin to talk softly, saying her name. Saying I'm fine and I love her. It's okay. Slowly I can feel her begin to relax and understand. She's coming back to herself.

Then the questions start: Did I have to pull my gun? Did I use it? Is everyone alive? Did I shoot the monster?

She's back.

I tell her how it all went down. She's full of more questions. This is good; she's getting the stress out now.

"When do I get to see you and touch you and make sure you're okay?"

"Hopefully later tomorrow. It all depends on how long the procedural stuff here takes. I still need to call George in Elko and tell him what happened. Then I should be able to take a few days off, I hope."

"If he doesn't let you off, I'll call his wife." That's my girl. Full of spunk.

Lou comes over to the car and tells me the "inquisitors" of the shooting team are ready for me. I explain I must talk to my undersheriff first. George can't be blindsided by anything.

George is beside himself with emotion. Almost as bad as my wife. "I was going to call up there several times today. I had to know what was going on. Thank God you're all right."

I give him the quick version of what happened, and now the Portland shooting team needs to interview me.

"Go ahead, but if they try to twist anything back on you, shut up and call me...I'll get on the next plane. You should be a hero there, not a suspect."

"Easy, George, I'm told they're fair guys and this is standard procedure."

"Yeah, yeah, I know. But all the same, let me know. When you're done you better take a few days and visit your lovely wife. You call her yet?"

"First thing, before you."

"Good husband. Let me know what's happening."

I meet the shooting team. They're low-keyed, going through the motions, crossing the t's and dotting the i's. This was a clear-cut self-defense situation and Lou has already given his account. They don't take long and wind up shaking my hand, slapping me on the back, and admiring my good shooting ability.

Then I'm on my way to the hospital with Lou to speak with Mr. Weaton. I hope he had a miserable ride. He's still in surgery when we arrive. But the prognosis is...he will survive. I want him alive. He needs to go to court and have the world hear what he has done to so many people's lives. Death would let him off too easy.

The Portland detective who rode with Weaton in the ambulance to the hospital said Weaton passed out on the way and said nothing further.

I need to ask him what he meant by *only one in California.* That bothers me. I know he's good for the woman's murder in San Jose. I investigated it and got the warrant. If he's acknowledging that one, why not the Morgan Hill case—*my case?* I know he was back on the road after his accident when it happened, and he was also in the area. His ex-wife verified it and the M.O. fits his pattern.

The good news, the Oregon highway patrolman Weaton shot is doing well. He had on a vest and that saved his life. He caught one bullet in his arm, but no serious damage. The vest took the other round; he'll only have a bruise. Weaton must have been aware his time was getting short. As the officer approached the truck, Weaton opened the cab door and fired two shots directly at him. Then drove off.

Lou and I go back to his office. He has reports to write and so do I. The hospital will call us when Weaton's out of surgery.

I call Greg in Enid, Oklahoma and advise him of Weaton's capture. He'll tell Gloria when she gets off work; they're still together. Greg tells me Arizona had Weaton's DNA sample. The Oklahoma crime lab was able to match it with DNA left on the lady who died in the hospital, in Gloria's arms. Another nail in Weaton's coffin.

I'm about to call my guys when my cell rings. "Charlie, I was just going to call you. Guess what?"

"Good job, son; I knew you'd get the S.O.B."

"Charlie, how the...how'd you find out so quickly?"

"Never underestimate Mr. Mayagi." He chuckles. "George just called me. You did me proud, my boy. Now when do the wife and I get to meet your new bride?"

"As soon as we can get her settled in Elko. You know, I've been kind of busy."

He laughs again. "I know, I know. But don't forget, you're like a son to us."

I'm getting choked up. I promise Charlie we'll all get together soon.

My cell rings again. Joseph, sure he knows by now. Thanks, George.

"So, boss, George told us. You shot the killer. You good?"

"I'm fine. Give your owl a fat field mouse for a treat. He was right on."

Gary gets on the other phone and we all have a good conversation. "You aren't going to stay up there, are you?"

"Hell no. It rains all the time here. I may not be fond of snow, but it does stop at times."

Lou takes a phone call. He motions to me. It's the hospital.

"Gotta go, guys; time to interview Weaton."

Lou drives us to the hospital. Weaton has come out of surgery, but things didn't go as well as expected. He's not doing well, so we need to hurry.

Weaton has numerous tubes and I.V.s coming out of various parts of his body. He's conscious and looks at me with his one remaining eye as we enter the room.

"You the cop who shot me?"

"I'm the cop whose been chasing your pathetic ass all over the country."

"You. You made those *flyers* in the truck stops. How did you know I'd changed my looks, my name; I couldn't get away from you. I had nightmares about you."

"Well, your nightmare is right in front of you. I have warrants for your arrest on two homicides, Arizona has another one, and Oklahoma has another. I'm sure there'll be several more before we're done. Oh, Oregon's not too pleased with you either."

He is weak. Speaking is difficult.

The nurse tries to get us to leave him alone. Lou takes her aside. Thanks, Lou, another good partner when I need one.

I take one more quick shot at my case. "Why did you say only one in California? I know there are two women dead there because of you."

Weaton tries to speak but his eye rolls back and the monitor next to the bed starts to scream.

"That's it! Out, out now," the nurse yells at us. She calls "Code Blue." Nurses, doctors, everyone comes pouring into the room as Lou and I slink out. We go to the waiting room.

"Think he'll make it?" Lou asks.

"No, he was fading when we came in. I could tell. I had to try to get something out of him. Damn! I wanted to hear it from him."

In a few minutes, a doctor comes out and tells us Weaton has passed. "He was pretty loaded on some drug, because we had a hell of a time keeping him under during the surgery. Otherwise, he should have survived. His blood count was also bad. I'd say he was riddled with cancer. Probably in a lot of pain."

His death allows various agencies with open homicides linked to Weaton's DNA to close their cases. It doesn't help the victims' families. I don't get the closure for them the press seems to think they need. To me losing a loved one cannot be mended or closed. If the responsible person is convicted—or in our case, killed—it still doesn't heal the loss. *My thoughts.*

I finish all I need to do in Portland. Lou takes me to the airport for a flight to the arms of my wife. I need to hold her and get myself back to earth. I am flooded with conflicting emotions. She'll soothe me and make it all right with the world again.

P.K. meets me at the Reno airport and after a long embrace and many tears we immediately go to her home. Inside packing boxes are stacked everywhere.

"Going somewhere?" I ask in an official tone.

"Yes, I am. I am moving to Elko to keep you out of trouble and save my sanity. I hate being so far away from you," she answers, just as officially.

Gotta love that girl; she's the best.

We stay in and cuddle up. She gets me unwound and I start to make sense of everything again. I've had pangs of guilt. I feared some people may have died because of my aggressive pursuit of Weaton. I know it was my job, but the guilt has been in the back of my mind the whole time I've been chasing him. P.K. points out Weaton knew he had to keep changing identities because of his need for a CDL. That wasn't my doing. She is correct and puts everything in such a logical manner it helps me let it go, somewhat.

"I talked to the man. He was so worried, he had nightmares about me."

"Well, good. You certainly lost sleep over him, it's only right you haunted him."

I reach over and give her a long kiss. "I love you, baby. I love you so much. You give me the emotional strength I need."

"Good. Now turn out the lights and come here," she purrs.

Chapter 43

My organized wife has all her business arrangements handled so she can transfer operations to her new office in Elko. While I have been out saving the world, she has packed her office, and with big brother's help, has it all loaded into a U-Haul truck. She has most of her clothes and personal items in boxes. This woman is on fire. I'm ready. Too long without her.

"When do you want to leave?" I ask.

"In the morning. I'm done here and need to get the office ready for my first patient next week. I've got a business to run. My patients depend on me."

"You already have an appointment set up for Elko? How'd you know I'd be back?"

"I *knew* you would be back. Besides, if you were still splashing around in Oregon my brother would have taken me."

"How would you get into the house?"

"I would have stayed with George and his wife. I've been talking almost daily with her."

"You are an amazing woman."

"*Your* amazing woman."

That settled, we head out the next day. I rented a trailer for her Jeep. She was planning to drive Baby, but I said we had been apart too long, and I would rather she be beside me for the long trip. No argument from P.K. She settles into the cab alongside me and we're off. It's an extremely long trip when driving a truck. But the weather's good, and we eventually make it to our home. We unload her belongings and then take the truck over to her office. On the door to her new office is a sign:

P.K. Kelly-Carson – Ocularist

"How'd you pull that off?"

"A good fairy helped me out." She smiles smugly.

Her office furnishings and files unloaded, the U-Haul turned in, and we are home at last!

The house is somewhat of a mess since I left in a hurry for Oregon, but it doesn't take long for us to get it all in order. I don't take up much closet space so she can get her things put away easily. Since it has been a long day we go out for a quick dinner and then home to bed. P.K. already has her day planned for tomorrow. Mine, too, I might add.

"You're still on leave, right? So you can help me get the office ready."

"Yes, dear," I say as I turn off the light. "*Come here*."

****

We spend the next few days getting her office completed and the house looking like a couple lives there, not a lonely bachelor. I didn't think it looked that bad before. Geeze.

Back at work I receive congratulations, cheers, etc. I have come to terms with the issues and am ready to close the door on that part of my life. It had become a large part of my life.

The department has made good use of the P.R. value of the case. Reporters want to interview me, and phone calls from other agencies are looking for a tie-in to their outstanding cases. I'm about ready to go back on leave, but George is great. He steps in and has all the calls and inquiries routed to his office. I appreciate this. I tell him I need to get back into the swing of things and will manage the calls later.

I talk with the Arizona Highway Patrol captain who handled Bennett's case, and of course, Greg, from Enid P.D. Gloria, Weaton's ex-wife is emotional about his death. Relieved he's no longer a threat but still, it's upsetting. Greg will be there to help; I have no doubt. While talking with him I mention how Weaton insisted he had only one killing in California. Greg said he'd dig further into Weaton's whereabouts after his accident and hospitalization. He'll see if Gloria can shed some light on the time frames involved. He confirms the date and time of "my case" in Morgan Hill.

Morgan Hill, my case. My mind goes back to what started it all. There was no physical evidence. Wait— DNA. We didn't know about it back then, but it is possible a trace of blood or something could be in the lab results from the coroner's report. It's a long shot, but worth an ask. I call the Santa Clara County Coroner's Office. Eventually I talk with the coroner. Unlike the TV image, he's a normal sounding guy. He listens to my request; says he'll dig into the files and see if perhaps anything useful is still there. He tells me not to get my hopes up. I ask about the clothing she was wearing. That would have been returned to the police department, he says.

Sure, I knew that. I call my old department and am referred to the chief detective. *More than one?* How things have changed. I have been gone awhile.

"Detective Green."

"Tom Green?"

"Yes, sir, Tom Green. Who is this?"

"Bob Carson, the reason you got hired."

"Bob, damn; it's good to hear from you. Can I have your autograph? You're quite the hero."

"Why, because you got hired?"

"No. Because you got the trucker who killed all those women. Everyone is talking about it. You're big-time news here."

"I had no idea it would be spread so far."

"Oh yeah, it's all over the news. The sheriff's making hay with it as you were *his* detective first. You know how politics are. So how are you; are you around here? I would sure love to have a beer and hear about the case."

"No, I'm in Elko, but I'll hold you to the beer next time I'm down there."

I tell Tom what I need. He remembers the old case, *my case.* He says he'll dig through the evidence storage and find the clothes. When he finds them, he'll send them to the crime lab and have a DNA check run. He confirms the date of the incident and I give him the case number.

"You kept that number? You unquestionably wanted to find him."

I give Tom a brief run-down and then let him go search. I advise the Santa Clara County coroner about the clothing and that Detective Green will be getting them to the crime lab.

After a few days' things begin to settle down. My ocularist is happy in her new office and has seen her first patient. Our house is a happy house. Love abounds throughout. We've been to Joseph's mom's for dinner and of course to George's several times. The wives get along great.

Joseph and Gary both seem to be staying with their respective ladies. We were worried about Gary, but the youth counselor seems up to the task. She has made a positive impact on him.

Mr. and Mrs. Carson are now to the point where we have people over to *our home* for dinner. Life is great.

One day the Santa Clara County Coroner calls me. He had all the samples from the victim's body retested, and has the results of the evidence Tom Green took in. Bless Tom, he didn't send it to the lab, he drove it in himself. I knew he would be a good cop.

Unfortunately, the coroner says there was no DNA except the victim's found on anything submitted. Dead end. No help there. Now Greg is my only hope. I want to call him but stop myself. He'll let me know when he has an answer. Gloria's memory is my biggest asset now.

Next, I receive a call from Lou in Portland. The autopsy is complete and Weaton died of complications resulting from a pneumothorax (the *sucking chest wound*), a combination of drugs in his system, and his weakened condition from cancer. According to the coroner, he probably had been in a lot of pain during his last weeks. Lou says no prescription medications were found in his apartment. He had apparently not seen a doctor for his pain. Maybe he didn't know what was wrong and just kept taking illegal drugs to feel better. Who knows?

****

The Carsons are happily going about their life

together. The new location seems to be working out for P.K. Business is back to what it was, and she is thrilled. She has time to paint in between appointments and has almost completed the Ruby Mountains for George's wife. I watch as it progresses toward a finished work of art. I'm in awe. My little artist is already discussing her next painting. There's even talk of putting her work in a local gallery. Thank you, George's wife. Could be fun for P.K.

When I least expect it, Greg calls from Enid. It's late afternoon. I'm at my desk finishing up some of the necessary evils of paperwork that come with the job.

"Greg, how's Gloria doing?" I stall. I don't feel comfortable about the call.

"Oh, she's fine now. It was a shock at first, but she's good." He's hesitating and stalling, too, I can tell.

"Uh...Bob, I don't know how else to say this, so here it is: Weaton was definitely not in Morgan Hill on the date of your case. He was in the hospital in Tulsa, Oklahoma having reconstructive surgery for his eye socket, so the prosthesis would fit properly. I double checked all the time frames. He was in the hospital a day before your date and remained for two days after. I don't know what else to say. I'm sorry, buddy. I know how much the case means to you."

I thank Greg and hang up. As I sit there feeling the emotions overwhelming me, I see the waning afternoon sun spill across my desk and toward the door. I take the hint. I get up, go through the door, and head home. I need my wife's comfort and strength.

I may not have closed this case yet, but following it led me to the love of my life.

A word about the author...

RJ Waters has lived the life the book portrays. He uses his imagination, interspaced with humor, to transform his real-world experiences in law enforcement, in the public and private sectors into a believable novel. Waters and his wife, Penny, live in Las Vegas.

Thank you for purchasing
this publication of The Wild Rose Press, Inc.

For questions or more information
contact us at
info@thewildrosepress.com.

The Wild Rose Press, Inc.
www.thewildrosepress.com